"DO YOU KNOW WHERE WE'RE GOING?" LUCY DEMANDED.

"Don't you remember?" asked Mary, genuinely surprised.

Lucy looked incredulously at her sister. "Me?! *You're* the one who set up this trip. Don't *you* remember where we're staying?"

Lucy glanced around, for the first time noticing their surroundings. The street was deserted. At least, it *seemed* to be. It was too dark to say for sure. The shadows down the street could have been garbage cans . . . or people crouched down, waiting to mug them.

Lucy felt fear shoot through her. She was on a New York City street, it was after midnight, and she was lost.

DON'T MISS THESE

7th Heaven

BOOKS!

AND COMING SOON

7th Heaven™

SISTERS THROUGH THE SEASONS

by Amanda Christie

An Original Novel

Based on the hit TV series
created by Brenda Hampton

Random House 🏠 New York

7th Heaven ™ & © 2002 Spelling Television Inc.
All rights reserved.
Produced under license by Random House, Inc.

All rights reserved under International and
Pan-American Copyright Conventions.
Published in the United States by
Random House Children's Books,
a division of Random House, Inc., New York,
and simultaneously in Canada
by Random House of Canada Limited, Toronto.

www.randomhouse.com/teens

Library of Congress Control Number: 2002102654
ISBN: 0-375-82290-9

Printed in the United States of America
First Edition
10 9 8 7 6 5 4 3 2

7ᵗʰ Heaven™

SISTERS THROUGH THE SEASONS

RUTHIE GOES TO HOLLYWOOD

ONE

Ruthie Camden was in love. It wasn't just any old love, either. It was real love. Far more passionate and beautiful than any love her siblings had ever known. Truer than the love her Mom and Dad felt for each other. Deeper than any ocean, higher than any mountain . . .

Ruthie shut her bedroom door and placed a chair under the doorknob, ensuring against unwanted visitors. Then she walked to her nightstand and opened the bottom drawer. Inside were a dozen glossy teen magazines, purchased with her allowance money. She pulled the newest one out, her heart pounding as she flipped to the center poster.

There he was. Him. Josh Kindle, the biggest teen hunk on television. Without him, what was there to live for?

The young man's dark eyes stared out from the pages as if they were reaching out to join her heart with his. His black hair was just messy enough to let Ruthie know that he tackled life with the same gusto she did. And his muscles . . . Nobody at school had muscles quite like that.

Ruthie turned the page and suddenly her heart stopped as she read the words that would change her life: The magazine was sponsoring a contest to meet Josh Kindle! The winner, chosen from a random drawing, would be flown to Hollywood for three nights—and while there, have a walk-on role on Josh's television show! How had she missed this page before?

Ruthie snatched a pen off her nightstand and flipped onto her stomach. She placed the form on her bed and began scribbling furiously. She would win this contest. She didn't doubt that for one moment. It was her fate. Their fate. After all, what force was powerful enough to stop true love?

· · ·

Two months later, the letter arrived. Ruthie rushed home from school as she'd done every day since entering the contest. There it sat on the kitchen table, unopened, with her name typed across it. The name of the teen magazine was in the upper left corner of the envelope.

"This is it!" she said aloud.

Ruthie picked up the letter and held it in her hands as though she were holding her very future. She closed her eyes and slid her finger beneath the lip of the envelope.

As she pulled out the letter, her eyes darted to the first sentence, which read:

CONGRATULATIONS, RUTHIE CAMDEN!
YOU'VE WON A TRIP TO HOLLYWOOD!

"No way!" she shouted, ecstatic.

Ruthie almost fainted as she continued to read, delighted to learn that it was no joke. She had really won the contest! Just as she had known she would. She was going to Hollywood. She was going to meet Josh Kindle. . . .

Just then, Ruthie's second-favorite hunk walked through the kitchen door. It was Robbie, her older sister Mary's ex-boyfriend, who rented a room at the

Camdens' rambling two-story home. He ruffled Ruthie's dark hair as he passed, then stopped.

"You're white as a ghost, Ruthie. What's wrong?"

Ruthie put her hand over her heart and dramatically closed her eyes. "Nothing's wrong—everything's right," she cooed, and held out the letter.

Robbie read it over and whistled, impressed. "Wow, this is big-time, Ruthie. Have you asked your parents if you can go?"

Ruthie grabbed the letter and rolled her eyes. "Please. I don't have to ask them. All I need is an adult chaperone—and I think *you* would be perfect."

Robbie laughed. "I'm not sure they would agree, although I'd love to go. Maybe you should ask them first."

"Ask who what?" came a voice from the hallway. Ruthie looked up and saw Mary bounding down the stairway with a basketball in hand. She was en route to the court outside.

Ruthie's eyes lit up at the opportunity to tell her big news. "I'm going to Hollywood. I've won a contest to meet Josh Kindle!"

Mary looked at her little sister skeptically. "*The* Josh Kindle? The one you talk about every minute of the day?"

Ruthie grinned and held out the letter as her other big sister, Lucy, walked in from the living room. Mary skimmed the letter as Lucy read over her shoulder. When she came to the word "chaperone," Mary held up her hands.

"No need to look any further, Ruthie— I'll be your chaperone. I've been needing a trip to Tinseltown anyway."

Lucy grabbed the letter away from Mary and scoffed. "You? Entrusted with the precious life of our little sister? Ha! You're not responsible enough to feed a dog, let alone keep Ruthie alive on the streets of Hollywood!"

Mary rolled her eyes. "I was made for Hollywood. Little innocents like yourself would get eaten alive. You don't know how to hail a cab, let alone chase down a robber."

Lucy put her hands on her hips. "I lived in New York City, I'd like to remind you."

Mary laughed. "And you came running home like a mouse in a cat house."

"You couldn't even survive in Buffalo," Lucy retorted.

Mary shook her head. "I was bored in

Buffalo. I didn't leave because I couldn't hack it."

"I didn't, either!" Lucy yelled, much to the enjoyment of all the observers now gathered in the kitchen. A fight between Lucy and Mary was better than the Super Bowl.

Just then, the Reverend Camden hurried in through the back door, his arms full of groceries. He stopped when he saw the flock of kids gathered in the kitchen.

"What's going on?"

Lucy handed her father the letter. "Ruthie's won a trip to Hollywood."

"*And* a walk-on role with Josh Kindle!" Ruthie shouted, spinning in circles across the tile floor.

"And *I'm* the chaperone!" shouted three different voices.

As the Reverend read the letter, a large smile crept across his face. "This is big news, Ruthie."

Ruthie stopped spinning and began jumping. "I know! Josh is the love of my life!"

The Reverend grinned again—his youngest daughter always made him smile. "I wish I could go with you. I love Hollywood. The boys from the band and I used to play a little gig on the Sunset Strip, back in the day." Then he shook his head sadly. "But I've got a conference to attend next weekend. Looks like this is a job for your mother."

Ruthie's heart sank. Her mother was the last person on Earth she wanted escorting her to Hollywood.

At that moment, Mrs. Camden straggled through the door from the laundry room. Her two youngest sons, Sam and David, were clinging to her legs, crying out for attention. She held a load of laundry in one arm and a cookbook in the other.

"Me?" she barked. "In Hollywood? Next weekend? Very funny!" She threw the laundry on the kitchen table, grabbed Mary by the ear, and pointed at it.

"Your turn."

As Mary began to protest, Mrs. Camden shoved the cookbook into the hand of Ruthie's brother Simon, who had just wandered in from upstairs. "Figure it out," she ordered, and pushed him toward the stove.

Then she fired her deadly gaze at Ruthie. "You can't go to Hollywood next weekend." She grabbed the letter and read the fine print. Her head was shaking. "And you *certainly* can't take next Friday off. You have the state achievement exams to study for. You're behind."

Ruthie began to protest, but her mother reached down and closed her mouth.

"And you know why you're behind?" she asked. "You're behind because you've been daydreaming about that silly TV star when you should be studying."

The Reverend put his arms around his wife, soothing her. "You need a vacation, Annie. And that's exactly what this will be. The letter says you'll stay at the nicest hotel in Hollywood. You'll have a limo driver. Free dinners at fancy restaurants. Massages."

Massages? Annie cocked her head, reconsidering. She looked down at the two boys yanking on her pants legs. She smelled the awful odor coming from Simon's corner of the kitchen. What was she waiting for?

TWO

At the Glenoak airport, Ruthie looked totally Hollywood as she opened the double glass doors and pushed her way inside, her hot pink sunglasses announcing her arrival. She attracted stares from every corner of the small building.

"Ruthie!" her mother shouted from outside the doors. But Ruthie kept walking, holding her fake cell phone to her ear as though she were attending to very important business. She already felt like a movie star, and loved the way people were looking at her. They could tell she was important.

Suddenly her mother grabbed her by the shoulder and spun her around. Mrs.

Camden pointed at a small blue bag that was sitting outside the double doors.

"That's your bag, Ruthie, and I'm not carrying it."

"But it's *terribly* ugly," Ruthie whispered.

"But it has your clothes in it," Mrs. Camden reminded her.

"I'll pay you to carry it," Ruthie begged.

Mrs. Camden was not amused. "I'm not your servant. Go get your bag right now."

Ruthie scowled and stormed off after the bag. She could already tell that her mother intended to ruin her trip. Didn't she realize that Ruthie was about to be a television star? That in less than two days, she'd be Josh Kindle's girlfriend? What kind of celebrity carried a beat-up old duffel bag? It didn't even have wheels on it. And it was powder blue, which was *so* passé.

She grabbed the bag and headed for her mother, who was now at the ticket counter. Ruthie sighed with an air of superiority. If she couldn't look like a TV star, she could at least act like one.

Ruthie sashayed over to the counter

and threw the bag down next to her mother's. She sighed again and looked at the attendant. "That's her bag," she said. "She just loaned it to me because mine was too big."

Mrs. Camden smiled at the woman, ignoring Ruthie's comment. "We're going to Los Angeles," she said as she handed the woman their tickets.

The woman nodded and typed on her keyboard. "You'll be on a propeller plane today," she informed them.

Mrs. Camden groaned. She hated those little planes. They made her sick to her stomach. "Why aren't we on a jet?" she asked.

The woman smiled. "Los Angeles is only a two-hour drive, with no traffic. Most people just drive because it's so expensive to fly such a short distance."

Ruthie stood on her tiptoes, put her hands on the counter, and made an overly loud declaration. "My TV show's budget covers all the expenses. Cost is not an issue."

The attendant was staring at Ruthie with a mixture of fascination and skepticism. "You're on a TV show?" she asked.

Ruthie sighed dramatically and nodded. "Have you ever heard of the show *Too Cool*?"

Mrs. Camden started to explain, but the woman chirped so loudly she wouldn't have been heard anyway. "Why, yes, I have! My daughter watches it all the time!"

Ruthie leaned over and whispered to the attendant. "Well, *I'm* on the show. That's why I'm hiding behind these glasses. I don't want anyone to recognize me."

Ruthie felt a tap on her shoulder. She turned to see a man standing behind her. "Did I hear you say that you're on the show *Too Cool*?"

Ruthie nodded, but this time Mrs. Camden prevailed, explaining that Ruthie wasn't a regular cast member. She had won a contest and was going to be a "day player." But the man was so excited that he wasn't listening. He was focused on Ruthie.

"My son absolutely loves the show. Could you autograph my luggage tag for him?"

Ruthie squealed in delight and took the tag. She began scribbling as Mrs. Camden further explained that Ruthie would only be in one episode. The man shrugged. As far as he was concerned, Ruthie was a star.

After Ruthie finished signing the tag, she leaned over and whispered in her mother's ear. "Perception is reality, Mom." Then she gave her a conspiratorial wink, which Mrs. Camden did not return.

"You better watch that ballooning head of yours," Mrs. Camden ordered. "I'll happily prick it if it gets much larger."

As the two started toward the gate, Mrs. Camden warned Ruthie that her walk-on role would be small. "I don't think they give big roles to people that haven't auditioned."

"But I'll have lines, right?"

"Don't expect them and you won't be let down."

Ruthie shrugged. She wasn't going for the acting anyway. "The only thing I expect is to meet Josh Kindle—and to have him fall head over heels in love with me!"

Mrs. Camden couldn't help but smile as she put her arm around Ruthie. She was happy to be here, especially with her youngest daughter. But she had no idea what to expect. Would the TV show treat them well? How would Ruthie behave?

When Mary and Lucy were Ruthie's age, everything was a struggle. They never wanted Mrs. Camden around. They felt as if everything she did was an interference in their lives. But who knew? Maybe the next few days would be smooth sailing?

Ruthie pushed her mother's arm off her shoulder and Mrs. Camden laughed.

"What?" Ruthie asked.

"Mary and Lucy used to do the same thing when they were your age. I don't take it personally anymore," Mrs. Camden explained.

Ruthie yawned, bored with her mother's observations. "Hey!" she suddenly said. "Can we drag the Sunset Strip? And see the Hollywood Walk of Fame? And shop in Beverly Hills? And—"

Mrs. Camden put her arm back around Ruthie and pulled her in. She kissed Ruthie's head, refusing to let her get away. "I know this is a very special vacation, Ruthie, but it happens to be right before your achievement exams. *And* you're missing school tomorrow. We'll be spending a lot of time at the hotel studying."

Ruthie sighed. Studying wasn't exactly what she had in mind. Ruthie smiled up at her mother, then firmly removed her arm. "Unless, of course, Josh wants to take me out on a date. . . ."

THREE

After a turbulent plane ride into Los Angeles, Mrs. Camden was delighted to be on solid ground again. Her stomach was in knots, her heart still lodged in her throat. Now she remembered why she hated traveling. She grabbed Ruthie, who was walking the wrong direction down the terminal. "This way, sweetheart."

Ruthie was gawking in amazement. There were people everywhere. People of every style and culture imaginable. More people in this one hallway than in her whole school combined. And she could tell by looking out the window that there were a lot of other hallways.

She slid her pink sunglasses up on top

of her head and stared at the fascinating people walking by. Maybe she was crazy, but it felt like everybody around her was beautiful. Like an airport full of movie stars. She'd heard Los Angeles was like this, but who knew that it was really possible?

"Mom!" Ruthie shouted, pointing at a tall man in a baseball cap. "That's . . . that's . . . I can't remember his name . . . but he's a movie star!"

Mrs. Camden pushed Ruthie's hand down into her pocket and hurried her along as the man smiled graciously. Ruthie's eyes were the size of quarters. Just as suddenly as he had appeared, the man was gone, lost in the sea of people.

As mother and daughter walked down the escalator toward the baggage claim, Mrs. Camden began eyeing the line of people before her, looking for someone. And then she spotted him: a distinguished-looking man in a suit and tie. He held a white card up that read:

ANNIE AND RUTHIE CAMDEN

Mrs. Camden waved at the man. He smiled and nodded, his salt-and-pepper hair perfectly matching his charcoal suit and white shirt. When they reached the bottom of the escalator, the man reached out to shake hands.

"I'm Richard," he said with a warm smile aimed at Mrs. Camden. "I'll be your driver for your entire trip. I have your itinerary and directions to every place you'll need to go. The limo is waiting outside."

He motioned them toward baggage claim. "Now let's grab your bags."

At the carousel, Ruthie spotted her ugly blue bag and had a grand idea. She could get Richard to carry it for her. It was his job! In fact, he was practically her servant! And she would be free to look like a Hollywood hipster.

She grabbed the bag off the belt and rushed up to him, sliding the glasses back on her olive-skinned face. "Could you take this? It's very heavy."

Richard nodded. "That's my job," he said, and gently took it from her arms. "What else do you need assistance with?"

"Will you open my door when I get into the limousine?"

"Of course I will."

"And close it, too?"

"Only the best for you and your mother."

Ruthie shook her head. "You don't

need to do anything special for her. She's not the contest winner, I am."

Richard pulled back in mock surprise. "Oh, is that right? So you're the princess and she's the maid. Is that how it goes?"

"Exactly!" Ruthie said.

Just then, Mrs. Camden walked up, lugging her bag. Richard reached down and took it from her.

"Hey!" Ruthie complained.

"Oh, no," Mrs. Camden began, fighting him for it. "You don't need to do that."

Richard smiled and untangled her fingers from the strap of the bag. "It would give me great pleasure to take your bag."

Ruthie's eyebrows suddenly arched. Was he flirting with her mother? She made a disgusted face. What an awful thought. Mrs. Camden smiled at him and released the bag. Ick.

As Richard led them outside, Ruthie leaned over and whispered to Mrs. Camden. "Somebody has a crush on an old married lady," she quipped.

Moments later, they were climbing into a limousine that was longer than three of the Camdens' vans put together. "It's the long kind!" Ruthie squealed to her mother.

Richard nodded as he began shutting the door. "It's called a stretch. It's the top of the line."

As they drove down the I-10 freeway toward Hollywood, Mrs. Camden was surprised at how crisp and clear the air was.

Richard explained that autumn in Los Angeles was the most beautiful time of the year. The rains cleared out the air, and visibility was higher than usual.

He pointed north to an ambling stretch of green and brown foothills. "Those are the Hollywood Hills," he explained. "We'll be right at their base in fifteen minutes, driving into your hotel."

"Where's the Hollywood sign?" Ruthie asked, leaning up over her seat to see out the window.

Richard's hand moved east and settled on a small white stretch of letters, just visible from the freeway. "East of the Cahuenga Pass," he said.

There it was, all right! Ruthie couldn't contain her excitement. How could she sit still in the back of a limousine? While heading straight toward Hollywood? It was all too much to handle.

Mrs. Camden smiled. She hadn't seen Ruthie this excited in a long time. Maybe ever. She reached over and squeezed Ruthie's knee.

As Richard exited the freeway, he pointed out a movie studio and explained that it was the oldest studio in the city. "We'll be visiting it tomorrow."

Ruthie rolled down her window and stuck her head out, staring at the gigantic arches and the old iron gate that stretched across them. "You mean we get to go inside there?"

Richard nodded. "That's where the set of *Too Cool* is."

Ruthie studied the archways, imagining Josh Kindle driving through them every morning. She bet he had a convertible. . . . But before her image was complete, the arches disappeared from sight as Richard turned left down Sunset Boulevard, where palm trees reached up toward the blue sky like the golden figure of the Academy Award.

As they pulled into the hotel, even Mrs. Camden couldn't deny her excitement. It looked like an old French castle hidden away in the foothills of the Sunset Strip.

They were really here. This was Hollywood!

Two bellhops, wearing all white, approached the limo and opened their doors. Richard walked around to the trunk and pulled out their bags, handing them off to the bellhops, who placed them on a silver cart and pushed them into the hotel.

Richard handed Mrs. Camden his business card. "I'm at your service. Any time you need me, call this number and I will be here within half an hour." Then he placed a neat stack of bills in her hand. "This is from the producer of the television show. It's to be used to tip the hotel staff. You should tip the bellhops, room service, laundry, everybody."

Mrs. Camden couldn't believe how big the pile was. It was hard for her to accept it.

"And you?" she asked. "Do I tip you, too?"

Richard shook his head no. "As I said, it is my great pleasure to assist you."

Ruthie stepped in between the two of them. Her tone, usually comic, was suddenly snappish and ungrateful. "Excuse me, Richard, but *I'm* the contest winner, remember? You're at *my* service."

Mrs. Camden's mouth dropped open. "Ruthie!"

Ruthie rolled her eyes. "I was joking!"

"I'm not so sure you were."

Richard smiled at Ruthie. "It's okay. I'm at your service, too." He turned back to Mrs. Camden. "Enjoy your dinner. I hear the ahi tuna is divine."

Mrs. Camden smiled. "Thank you. It sounds absolutely wonderful."

Richard turned and winked at Ruthie. "And for you, there is nothing finer than the Grande Dame Cheeseburger. It's superb."

Mrs. Camden put her hand on Ruthie's shoulder, her excitement building. "I can't wait another minute. Let's check in!"

FOUR

Ruthie felt like royalty. The hotel was even better than she had imagined. The two beds were so high she had to jump to get onto them. And they each had their own silver canopy frames, just like in all the old movies. Gauzy white fabric draped down from the canopy to the floor, skirting the entire frame of the bed.

And everything was white. The lounge chair, the ottoman, the love seat, the beds, the pillows. White, white, white, as far as the eye could see. That is, except for the silver.

There were shiny silver lamps and mirrors and hair dryers. There was even a silver TV! It was all just incredibly cool. Who would have thought to make an entirely silver and white hotel? Even room service had arrived wearing white uniforms with silver piping along the sleeves. And Ruthie's Grande Dame Cheeseburger was served on a silver platter with a white linen napkin.

Ruthie sat on the bed, eating her burger. Richard was right. It *was* good. It was listed on the menu for twenty-two dollars. *Twenty-two dollars! For a cheeseburger!* Why, that was enough money to buy two CDs on sale. At McDonald's, you could get a cheeseburger for a dollar. Which meant this cheeseburger was worth twenty-two McDonald's cheeseburgers!

Ruthie savored the taste of money in her mouth. Then she wondered what her mother's tuna must taste like. It cost thirty-four dollars! She must be in heaven right now, Ruthie thought, looking over at her mother. And none of that money came out of the Camden bank account. *That* was a beautiful thing!

As Ruthie munched, she wondered what else she could get with her enormous supply of money during the next three days. She intended to spend. To shop and dress like a star. She lifted up her cheeseburger to take a bite, and suddenly had a great idea.

"Careful!" Mrs. Camden said, pointing to a long, cheesy string of juice that was about to drip off the bun. "Don't get that on the comforter."

But that was exactly what Ruthie had in mind. "Duvet," she corrected her mother as the thick strand stretched ever closer to the bed.

"I don't care what you call it," Mrs. Camden said, her voice becoming more urgent. "Just be careful with your Grande Dame Cheeseburger."

Ruthie grinned at her mother, then squeezed her burger as hard as she could. A stream of juice dropped dramatically on the white comforter, soiling it orange and brown.

Mrs. Camden jumped up, angry. "Now, why did you do that? I just told you not to!"

Ruthie raised an eyebrow and picked up the phone. "To test out laundry service."

Mrs. Camden was steaming as Ruthie requested laundry assistance. "We'll need it laundered and returned by 9 P.M.," Ruthie ordered. "I have to get my beauty rest."

As they waited for someone to arrive, Mrs. Camden watched Ruthie, who was reclining against several goose-down pillows. As a matter of fact, Ruthie had taken her mother's pillows to make herself more comfortable! Ruthie's legs were crossed, and she held her glass of Coke up in the air as if it were a sparkling glass of champagne. Her pinky finger was sticking up and out in a display of snobbery, and she was completely unconcerned about the work she had caused for the laundering staff. *Is that my child?* Mrs. Camden wondered, astonished.

In moments, the laundryman was at their door to pick up the duvet. Ruthie was enormously impressed, and grabbed a five-dollar bill from her mother's wad of cash. "Like I said, I need this before bedtime!" she demanded, shoving the cash in his hand and shooing him out of the room.

Mrs. Camden was frozen on the bed, studying her daughter. "Laundering costs money, Ruthie."

"Not ours!" Ruthie exclaimed flippantly as she opened the dessert menu. "Now, what would you like for dessert, Madame? There's tiramisu, crème brûlée, chocolate raspberry torte. . . ."

Mrs. Camden leaned over and shut the menu. "I'm not so sure you're having dessert."

Ruthie looked at her mother, confused. "But it's free."

"You're acting like a spoiled brat, and you haven't even arrived at the set yet. If this behavior continues, you won't be going at all. You'll be going home."

"What behavior? I'm just enjoying my free trip!"

"It may be free for you, but somebody is paying for it. And you need to respect that."

Ruthie rolled her eyes. "Somebody with lots of money. And every time we spend money, we're giving it to someone else. That laundryman needed that five dollars. That's the beauty of capitalism. The more we spend, the better the world is. I'm just helping out the economy."

Mrs. Camden narrowed her eyes at Ruthie. "You're indulging yourself in an irresponsible and selfish way. I told you not to spill on the comforter, and you did."

"Duvet."

"I'm serious, Ruthie."

Ruthie leaned back against her pillows and studied her mother's face, her eyes narrowing. Then she shook her head. "You wouldn't send me home. Not when you have free dinners, limos, and Richard at your beck and call—"

Mrs. Camden grabbed the phone. "I'll call Richard right now to drive you home. I'll stay here by myself."

Ruthie watched her mother's eyes as she dialed, trying to ascertain if she was bluffing. There was a vein popping out along her temple. Oh, yeah, she was serious. Ruthie reached over and hung up the phone.

"Okay, okay! Jeez! I was just having a little fun with my newfound power. I'll change my wicked ways."

Mrs. Camden looked at Ruthie. "I know that all of this is very exciting for you. But you need to understand something, Ruthie. Happiness doesn't come from money, and power. Some of the most unhappy people in the world are the people who can stay in this hotel anytime they want. It concerns me that you don't see that."

"What makes you think I don't see that?"

"Your behavior. The way you dressed today, the way you treated—"

"What's wrong with how I dressed?"

Mrs. Camden smiled and patted the bed next to her. But Ruthie shook her head. She wanted to stay right where she was. Alone. Facing off with her mother.

"There's nothing wrong with how you dressed. What's wrong is *why* you dressed the way you did."

"So now you're going to tell me you know why I do what I do?" Ruthie laughed and rolled her eyes.

Mrs. Camden nodded. "You dressed that way to make other people think that you were more important than them, that you were 'above' them. And being 'above' somebody is not something that a good person aspires to."

Ruthie thought about what her mother had said. Was there any truth to it? She shrugged. "I just like to be cool. I'm a cool cat."

Mrs. Camden laughed. "I know that. You're a very cool cat, Ruthie. And I also know that adolescence is the most important time to be 'cool.' But I want you to realize that 'coolness' can be an illusion. I especially want you to realize this while you're in Hollywood."

"Why in Hollywood?"

"Because Hollywood is the epitome of cool. Many people come here trying to be somebody they're not. I want you to try and look behind the 'illusion' of celebrity and see if you can see the real people behind the masks."

Ruthie was confused. "The masks?"

"Tomorrow, when we go on set and you meet your idols, I want you to try and treat them like people, not like 'stars.' They're no better than you, and you're no better than them. What people truly want is friendship, and love, and honesty. So try to give those things and I think you'll be surprised at what you get back."

Ruthie furrowed her brow. She felt like she was talking to a wizard. Like her mother was speaking in riddles. Whatever. She was just psyched to meet Josh!

Suddenly an ad on the television caught her eye. "Rad! The Teen Tube Awards are on Saturday night!" Just then, a picture of Josh flashed across the screen.

"He's up for the Hottest Hunk Award, Mom!"

Mrs. Camden sighed and opened Ruthie's social studies book. Ruthie hadn't heard a word she'd said. She reached over and turned off the TV. "You'll be studying Saturday night. Maybe Dad can tape it."

Ruthie groaned and fell back on her bed. How had she gotten stuck with the lamest mother on the planet?

FIVE

Bright and early the next morning, the limousine pulled through the arches of the famous movie and television studio. Ruthie sat quietly in the backseat, too nervous to do anything else. Richard rolled down his window and greeted the guard at the security island. The guard checked Richard's ID, cross-referenced it with a list on his computer, and then hit a button to open the gate.

Richard drove along a small road that was decorated on both sides with lovely trees and flowers. After several minutes, he pulled up in front of a charming bungalow, where an elderly man in a dapper suit stood smiling. There was a small red flower in his jacket's buttonhole.

"That's Edgar," Richard said. "He's the producer of the show, and he'll be your guide." Richard turned around and looked them both in the eyes. "You don't know how lucky you are to spend the day with Edgar Weiss. He's one of the most famous television producers in the world. And from what I hear, a very nice man."

Seconds later, Edgar was at their door, helping Mrs. Camden out and greeting Ruthie with her own *Too Cool* baseball cap.

"Wow! Rock on!" Ruthie exclaimed, and pulled the cap down over her long brown hair.

Edgar handed Mrs. Camden the red flower. "A beautiful rose for a beautiful lady."

Mrs. Camden blushed and thanked Edgar as he motioned them down the winding path. "Shall we head over to the set?"

"Yeah!" Ruthie exclaimed.

As the threesome walked along the narrow road, Ruthie was surprised at how cozy the studio was. There were many old cottages like Edgar's, and inside she could see people at computers writing, and others lounging in chairs reading scripts. There were gardens and even a big water fountain with a long bench in front of it. Was this where the stars hung out?

"So," Edgar began, addressing Mrs. Camden. "I hear your husband is a minister?"

"That's right," Mrs. Camden said. "He probably would have come today, but he had a conference to attend. I guess I'm lucky for that."

Edgar smiled and nodded. "My brothers are both rabbis. In fact, I almost became a rabbi myself. But I fell in love with television, and with the dream of using it to do great things for children." He laughed at himself. "I'm not so sure I've succeeded."

"So you've always produced children's television?" Mrs. Camden asked.

"Ah, yes! I love it!

Ruthie was beginning to get annoyed with all the adult talk. Where was the real action? The celebrities?

Then Ruthie froze. The dog from *Too Cool* was trotting by, right before her very eyes. And the dog's trainer was jogging after it, holding its leash. The woman waved at Edgar, who waved back.

"Left the doggie biscuits in the car!" she called as she ran by.

Ruthie tried not to act too starstruck. After all, it was just a dog. But she had to admit, it was pretty cool walking along the same path that Rocket trotted along every day.

Suddenly Ruthie heard a buzzing sound behind her. She turned around and saw a middle-aged man driving a little white golf cart. A sign that read JOSH KIN-DLE was attached to the windshield.

Ruthie felt her heart stop. Sitting in the passenger's seat was . . . Josh!

As the cart zipped by them, Ruthie tried to catch Josh's eye. But he just stared off in the distance. Ruthie turned around to follow the cart, but it disappeared around another bend in the road.

"That was Josh!" Ruthie exclaimed to her mother.

Edgar nodded, "Yes, it was. We're almost at the soundstage. Take a left where he did and you'll see stage twelve straight ahead."

Ruthie ran around the bend in the road and found herself in front of a big, square building. The number "12" was drawn across it in large, bold black letters. And there was Josh, climbing out of the cart! Ruthie wanted to shout to him, but knew that she couldn't. Not yet. Not until official introductions had been made.

She watched him swing open the door to the building, his black hair shining in the sun. Her heart was pounding. Just as the door closed behind him, a red light came on and began spinning around like a light on a police car.

"What is that?" Ruthie asked, trying to maintain her composure.

"That means they're shooting," Edgar explained.

"Shooting?" Mrs. Camden asked.

"It means the cameras are rolling and that we can't enter until the light goes off. If we went in now, we would disrupt the sound and they'd have to cut the take."

Ruthie suddenly realized that her hands were dripping with sweat. Her knees were even a little wobbly. How could just the *sight* of somebody do something so powerful? She took a deep breath and looked up at Edgar.

"Does Josh have a girlfriend?"

Edgar chuckled. "Not this week."

As quickly as it had flashed on, the light went off, and Edgar opened the door. "Watch your step. It's going to seem dark while your eyes adjust."

Sure enough, Ruthie could barely see and tripped over an extension cord that someone had forgotten to tape down. Edgar gave her a hand and then helped Mrs. Camden inside.

Once inside, Ruthie took in the sight of the stage. She couldn't believe how big it was. How high the ceilings were. And all the building materials that were strewn everywhere. There were so many fake walls propped up that it was like a maze. An endless maze of dark hallways with no people. Where was everyone?

Edgar led them down a hallway, between the actual soundstage wall and the back side of one of the many fake walls. "Those are called flats," Edgar explained.

Suddenly there was a doorway in one of the flats and Edgar turned into it. Ruthie and Mrs. Camden followed.

Ruthie let out a gasp. They were standing inside Josh Kindle's TV bedroom! It was exactly like she had seen it on the show!

There was his CD player, and his hockey stick next to his trash can, and the pop-star poster above his bed. It was all right here. She could reach out and touch it.

"Go ahead," Edgar said. "Just don't move anything. This is a hot set."

"A hot set?" Mrs. Camden asked.

"It means all the props are in place for shooting the next scene and can't be moved."

Ruthie touched the hockey stick, knowing Josh had picked it up many times on the show. His fingerprints were probably all over it. She closed her eyes and imagined it in his hands.

Then Edgar tapped her shoulder and motioned her through another doorway, which should have led into his bedroom hallway. But it didn't. It just led to more construction zones!

Edgar entered another doorway, and suddenly they were in the school cafeteria! And just across the way, Ruthie could see Josh's TV living room. It was so incredible that she almost had to rub her eyes—all of these rooms fit inside this one stage. Who would have thought?

Edgar put his hand up to his mouth to

indicate they should be as quiet as possible. Then Ruthie noticed that a red light on a wall nearby was flashing. Somewhere nearby, Josh was shooting a scene.

And that's when she heard his voice. Very faint, but definitely Josh's voice. Edgar began tiptoeing down the hallway, Ruthie and Mrs. Camden following. The sound of Josh's voice was drawing nearer. . . .

Ruthie could see a large crowd of people gathered around something, or someone, up ahead. There were three big cameras with men moving them back and forth. A woman was holding a huge microphone that stretched high over the crowd of people. Several crew members sat in director's chairs, hovering around a small television monitor.

"That's the director," Edgar whispered, pointing to a man directly in front of the monitor. "Everything the camera is recording right now is fed onto that monitor. So they're watching the scene on the TV, making sure it's framed appropriately and that the angles make sense."

"But . . . ," Ruthie began.

Edgar cut her off with a grin. "But where's Josh?" he whispered. "He's in that room, but you won't be able to see him until they call cut. Then all the people will scatter and we'll get closer so you can see."

Edgar pulled Ruthie in close to the TV monitor and Ruthie smiled. She could see Josh on the screen. He was in the burger joint, hanging out with his TV sister, the teen star Roxanne Bridges. Wow! She was going to get to see both of them today!

Suddenly Josh messed up a line. Angry, he jumped up and kicked the table, cursing. The director yelled, "Cut!"

All the people began to disperse as the director strode toward the room where Josh was sitting.

Now Ruthie could see clearly into the small room. There he was. . . . Ruthie took a deep breath.

He was arguing with Roxanne. Suddenly the actress threw up her hands and stormed out of the room, walking straight in Ruthie's direction. "Josh is such a jerk!" she cried to no one in particular. "He messed up his line, and then blamed it on me! I'm so over this!"

Ruthie looked at Edgar, about to ask him if what Roxanne said was true. But before she could get a word out, a woman wearing a headset whisked Ruthie away.

"Ready for your big role, kiddo?" she asked, as she plopped Ruthie down in a makeup chair.

"Uh . . . yeah," Ruthie began.

"I'm the assistant director, sometimes called the A.D.," the woman said, talking so fast Ruthie could barely keep up. "Here are your lines."

The woman handed her a page from a script. There were three lines highlighted. "Memorize this. I'll be back to get you in thirty!"

Ruthie grinned. "You mean I have lines?"

But the A.D. had already rushed off. Ruthie looked up at the flamboyant man that now stood above her with a makeup brush in hand. "Darling, you are gorgeous," he said. "That olive skin, that shiny hair. I'm going to turn you into an absolute star."

Meanwhile, Mrs. Camden was sitting in Edgar's director's chair when craft services walked by with a tray of goodies. "Chocolate cake?" the woman asked. "Cinnamon roll? Fruit platter?"

Mrs. Camden requested the cake and

was amazed at how rich it was. She looked around the set, surprised that everyone was so friendly. It was like a little family. Everybody knew everybody else. And everybody treated the visitors like honored guests. There were even arguments, just like in a family. Maybe Hollywood wasn't as bad as she'd thought?

The kids seemed a little out of control, though. "Why do you coddle these kids so much?" she asked, looking up at Edgar.

Edgar shook his head. "We shouldn't, but they have so many contractual rights that we have to. If they don't get what they want, they can walk right off the set."

"And what happens then?"

Edgar sighed. "There's no show."

SIX

Ruthie stared at herself in the vanity mirror. She looked like a movie star. There was no denying that. Unfortunately, she didn't feel like one. What if she couldn't remember her lines? What if she couldn't act? What if Josh laughed her off the set? He hadn't even noticed her, and she'd been on set for almost an hour. . . .

The assistant director ran up and squeezed her shoulder quickly. "Two minutes. Let's hear your lines."

Ruthie took a deep breath and looked down at her script page. But before she could read a single word, the woman grabbed the sheet. "No cheating I'll feed them to you."

Ruthie nodded, trying to look relaxed. But she wasn't relaxed at all. As the A.D. read Josh's line, which preceded Ruthie's, Ruthie closed her eyes and concentrated.

"You messed up my pizza order," the woman said, mimicking Josh.

Ruthie opened her eyes and smiled, pretending to be a teen waitress. "You wanted pepperoni. This is pepperoni."

The woman put her hands on her hips. "Yes, but I wanted extra cheese."

Ruthie pretended to point at a pizza. "And there it is. Lots of it."

"If you call that extra, then I'm calling you a moron."

Ruthie gritted her teeth and curled her hands into fists, pretending to be angry. "And I'm calling the manager to get you thrown out of here. Nobody talks to me like that!"

The A.D. smiled and nodded her head. "Wow, Ruthie. Not bad. Not bad at all. If you could throw a little more anger into your last lines, you'll be perfect. Now let's get you acquainted with Josh."

The woman put her arm around Ruthie and nudged her out of the makeup chair. She could sense Ruthie's anxiety.

"Don't be nervous. You'll be awesome."

As they approached, Josh was leaning against a wall playing a handheld electronic game. Ruthie felt her knees begin to get weak again. Why was this happening? Why couldn't she just relax? She was going to be a total geek in front of him!

"Josh, meet Ruthie Camden," the assistant director said. "She'll be playing the teen waitress."

Ruthie smiled shyly and held out her hand to shake. But Josh didn't even look up from his game. "Hey," he mumbled, completely uninterested. Then he glanced up at a passing man with a cart of food. "I need some water. Bottled. Flat. Now."

The man nervously shook his head. "I've only got food in my cart."

Suddenly Josh's soft dark eyes flashed with anger. "I don't care what you've got!" he shouted at the man. "Go get me some water!"

The man nodded and scurried off.

Ruthie felt sick. Roxanne was right. Josh really was a jerk!

"Listen, Josh," the woman started. "You and Ruthie need to go over your lines. She's the contest winner I told you about, and she needs to practice. . . ."

Josh scoffed. "A contest winner? I have to act with a contest winner?" Josh finally looked at Ruthie. "You're not a real actress, you're just some lucky kid who got your name pulled out of a hat. You don't deserve any lines."

Ruthie felt her face turning red with embarrassment. But she also felt anger bubbling up from deep within her.

"I've had to work to get to where I am," Josh continued. "I've been working since I was three years old—practically my whole life. Trying to get commercials, trying to get agents, and managers, and entertainment lawyers. Trying to pay for my mother's whims and my brother's braces and my sister's modeling classes. I deserve to be here—but you don't."

Ruthie took a deep breath, wishing she could be anywhere else at this moment. "You're right . . . ," she began. "I haven't worked to get here. But I entered the contest because I'm such a big fan of the show. I'm a big fan of yours, actually. . . ."

She couldn't believe she had been brave enough to admit that. She had basically just admitted she had a crush on him.

"Who isn't a fan of mine?" he scoffed.

Ruthie felt the redness in her cheeks deepen. All the confidence she had felt her entire life suddenly slipped away. Why did this boy have the power to make her feel so small? Because he was a celebrity?

Suddenly the words of Mrs. Camden came back to her.

When we go on set and you meet all your idols, I want you to try and treat them like people, not like stars.

Ruthie realized she wasn't treating Josh like a real person at all. She wasn't being honest. The real Ruthie was mad. Maybe if she reacted honestly, she would win his respect?

Ruthie put her hands on her hips and looked Josh right in the eyes. "You're about to lose a fan real fast."

Astounded, Josh took a step back. "You can't talk to me that way."

"Why can't I? You're no better than I am. You're just a boy who happens to be on TV. Big deal."

"I'm no better than you?" he laughed. "Then why do you watch my show every Friday night?"

Ruthie raised an eyebrow. "Maybe I'll

never watch it again. Maybe your ratings will drop and your show will be canceled."

Josh rolled his eyes. "Like losing one stupid fan will affect our ratings. I bet you don't even have a Nielsen's box, do you?"

"A what?"

Josh started laughing again. "Let's just say that nobody will even know you stopped watching. The show will go on and I will continue to make money and fans—and you'll continue to be a nobody."

Ruthie bit her lip. He was winning this argument, and fast. She was desperate. "Well . . . ," she struggled, "I could start a letter-writing campaign. I could get your contract nixed."

Josh laughed at the innocence of Ruthie's thought. "Contracts don't get nixed unless both parties are in agreement. And all the clauses are on my side. I have the most powerful attorney in the city. But even if I didn't, the network would never take a chance on losing me."

Ruthie felt powerless. She didn't even understand what he was talking about. He sounded like a businessman, not a teenager.

"I'm the biggest draw of the show," he

continued, his face getting redder as his voice rose. "I make money for the network bigwigs. Millions and millions of dollars. I am their job security. But if they don't start treating me better . . ."

Josh looked around the set. When he saw Edgar, he shouted loudly, "If you don't get this stupid girl off my set, I'll leave!"

Suddenly the whole set fell deadly silent. Was Josh serious? Would he actually stop production of the show just because he didn't want Ruthie there?

At that moment, Ruthie didn't care. She leaned right into Josh, her face red like his, her voice rising. "Stupid girl? I'll have you know I'm the smartest girl at my school. You live in a fantasy world, Josh Kindle. All these people do everything you ask, but that doesn't mean they like you. How could they? You're a tyrant. You order them around like slaves!"

From her director's chair, the actress Roxanne Bridges started clapping. But nobody else joined in. Mrs. Camden was holding her breath. Anxious as she was, she was very proud of her daughter.

Ruthie took a step back and threw up her hands. "I don't care if you throw me off the set. I don't need to be a TV star to feel cool."

Ruthie looked at her mother and motioned toward one of the exit doors. "Come on, Mom."

Just as Mrs. Camden started to get up, Edgar stood. "Neither of you is going anywhere. You are our guests, and Josh will treat you both with respect."

Josh's mouth dropped open in shock. He glared at Ruthie, then at Edgar. And then he uttered the last words any of them wanted to hear—the words that meant, in TV lingo, "we're done for the day." "This is a wrap!"

He walked off the set, disappearing out the nearest exit door.

Ruthie, Mrs. Camden, and the entire cast and crew sat for a long moment in silence. There was still so much work to be done, and yet they couldn't do it. That meant they had to catch up tomorrow. But what if Josh refused to return to work tomorrow, too? And next week? How would the show go on?

Edgar sighed and looked at everyone. "You heard the kid. It's a wrap."

They all stood up and began assembling

their belongings. Grips dismantled lighting equipment, cameramen unfastened their lenses and shrunk their tripods, and sound-board operators unplugged their many cables. Roxanne passed by Ruthie and smiled.

"I've wanted to say that for a long time. Thanks."

Ruthie smiled in thanks at the actress. It was a nice thing to say, and even better to hear. Yet deep down, Ruthie felt awful. She had caused a lot of problems for every-body.

Edgar put his arm on her shoulder and looked down at her. To her relief, he smiled. "You got spunk, kid."

SEVEN

Ruthie and Mrs. Camden sat on a leather couch in Edgar's office, waiting for him to finish a phone call. Ruthie needed to be close to her mother, and curled up next to Mrs. Camden. What if *Too Cool* was canceled because of everything she had said to Josh?

Edgar hung up the phone and turned his undivided attention to the Camdens. "Listen, Annie, Ruthie . . . I'm really sorry for the way Josh behaved today. For the way he treated you. And I'm especially sorry that you didn't get your walk-on role after coming all this way—"

Mrs. Camden interrupted him, amazed that he was apologizing. "Please don't apologize. We've had a wonderful trip, and have been so fortunate to meet someone like you. I'm very proud of Ruthie, but we both feel awful that you had to cancel production for the day."

Edgar shrugged. "You know what? This crew has been working nonstop since the day the show started. We've been breaking union rules left and right with overtime. They needed a break."

Mrs. Camden was glad to hear this, but she didn't entirely believe that Edgar's optimism was real. "What if Josh refuses to show up Monday? Can his lawyers shut down production indefinitely?"

Edgar nodded. But before Mrs. Camden could sigh, he held up his hand. "I saw this day coming over a year ago. Josh's ego is too big for his own good. Something had to give somewhere. I don't know. . . . Maybe we'll recast him."

Ruthie thought about what the show would be like without Josh. She shook her head, sad. It wouldn't be the same. Josh might be a real jerk, but he was talented. Without him, there would be no show.

A heavy silence settled over the room as they all thought about the situation.

Mrs. Camden was watching Edgar closely. She was certain there was something else on his mind. Something deeper than concerns about money and ratings.

"What are you really thinking, Edgar?"

The old man looked out the window at a citrus tree. Sunlight had turned the lemons a bright, shining gold. He smiled, but there was a sadness in his voice that contradicted the look on his face.

"I'm worried about Josh," he admitted. "He may be a thorn in everybody's side, but the kid's only fifteen. He has all the money and fame that anyone could want, but he's not happy. He doesn't have any friends. Not real ones, anyway. Some people say fame is a golden cage, and there's a lot of truth to that."

Edgar shook his head and sighed. "Even his mother is more concerned about his salary than his well-being. The kid's got nobody."

He turned back from the window and leaned back in his chair. "The last thing I want to do is get rid of him, or go to court—but how do you get through to a kid with so much power? He doesn't trust anybody. And why should he? He knows that I will always put the well-being of the show before his well-being. I'm just using him like everybody else."

Mrs. Camden started to protest when there was a knock on the door. A young production assistant stuck his head inside.

"Hey, Edgar. Josh wants to see Ruthie."

Ruthie sat up, surprised. In fact, everybody was surprised—Edgar more than anyone.

"He's still on the lot?"

"He's in his trailer," the P.A. said. "Can I take Ruthie over?"

Mrs. Camden nodded and started to get up. But Ruthie shook her head, certain that she needed to face Josh alone. "I'm not a little kid anymore, Mom. I need to do this on my own."

Mrs. Camden nodded, and Ruthie followed the production assistant out of the office.

As Ruthie and the P.A. zipped down the winding pathways in their little golf cart, Ruthie thought again about what her mother had told her in the hotel.

I want you to try and look behind the 'illusion' of celebrity and see if you can see the real people behind the masks.

Suddenly Ruthie realized what her mother had meant when she used the word 'mask.' All this time, she'd been seeing Josh as a completely different person than he really was. She wasn't seeing him, she was seeing what all the teen magazines and TV shows wanted her to see. She was seeing the mask that they had created. They wanted her to see Josh Kindle as a hunk, an object; not as a flawed, lonely human being.

Ruthie smiled as she thought about the phrase "illusion of celebrity." It *was* an illusion! This whole place—the fake sets, the makeup, the costumes—none of it was real. It was like somebody had worked a magic trick on Ruthie, tricking her into seeing something that wasn't really there.

As Ruthie climbed out of the cart and started up toward Josh's trailer, she felt her confidence return. Josh was no different than any of the boys she went to school with—and Ruthie had never been intimidated by them. So why was she still nervous?

The P.A. rapped on the trailer door, poked his head inside, then motioned

Ruthie up the stairs. As Ruthie climbed the steps, the P.A. pointed to the cart. "I'll be right out here if you need me."

Ruthie nodded, took a deep breath, and entered the trailer.

Inside, she was surprised to find a big, cold, empty room. Josh was sitting at a table, alone, with a social studies book open in front of him. It was the same book Ruthie studied! Was he actually doing the same schoolwork as her, even though he was two years older?

As if he were reading her mind, Josh shut the book, frustrated. "I'm not a very good student," he said. "It's hard to study when you work so much."

Ruthie nodded, realizing that what he said was probably true. She had never thought about that before: he had a full-time job, even though he was just a kid. How did he find time to study? "Do you work all day, every day?" she asked.

He shrugged. "Five to ten hours a day. Which is illegal because I'm a minor." He scoffed. "But who cares? I'm making money, right?"

Ruthie knew he was being sarcastic, because she used the same sense of humor when she wanted to avoid a sensitive topic. She smiled. "Well, if it helps any, I hate social studies, too."

She watched his face, hoping he would smile, but he didn't. He was looking out the window of his trailer, which looked straight into a soundstage wall. Ruthie shook her head, imagining him spending all his free time in this dreary trailer.

"So," she said, trying again. "Why are you still here if you're so mad at everybody?"

Josh shrugged. "Because my driver isn't here yet and my Mom's in Mexico."

"Your driver? You mean, you don't have a license?"

"I'm fifteen."

Ruthie couldn't believe that he didn't have his own car. It was hard to imagine him following the same laws that she did.

"Well, what about your dad? Can't he pick you up?"

Josh laughed, full of scorn. "That loser? He left us when I was a kid. Never called. Now that I'm famous, he won't stop calling. He just wants my money. He's even been to court to see if the judge will give him control of my trust."

Ruthie bit her lip, her nervousness returning. She wasn't getting very far with him. And he used all these inside business words that she didn't understand. He was like a brick wall, impossible to break down.

"So . . . why did you want to see me? I thought you hated me."

Josh finally looked at her, and his eyes were confused. "I don't know . . . I . . . just did." He struggled to explain. "I felt like we had a real conversation today."

"A conversation? I think it was a fight."

He nodded and looked down. "Yeah, but nobody's ever told me the things that you did. Everybody's afraid of me. Nobody's had the courage to tell me the truth about myself. I'm a jerk. Just like my dad. That's why nobody likes me."

"Of course people like you," Ruthie said.

He shook his head and looked straight at her. "Now *you're* being dishonest. You don't have to lie to me or feel bad for me. It's like you said: People like what I have. But you . . . you don't care about those things, do you?"

Ruthie smiled and admitted something. "I did. In fact, they were all I could think about when I left Glenoak to come here. But now that I'm here, well, it's still very exciting and fun . . ."

"But . . . ?" Josh prompted.

"Don't get me wrong, there are nice people and beautiful buildings and great food—" Ruthie bit her lip. She didn't want to offend him.

He smiled. "You can be honest."

"But it can also be a little, well . . . tense."

Josh laughed. "Tense. That's the understatement of the year!"

Ruthie reached out and took Josh's hand, surprised at her rising confidence. "You know what? Underneath all that anger, I know there's a good person waiting to get out, Josh. In fact, I can see that person right now."

Suddenly Josh sat upright, the sadness in his eyes turning to excitement. "I have the best idea!"

It was the first time Ruthie had seen him smile, and he looked so adorable, and handsome. Just like the character he played on TV. "Well, what is it?"

He took her hand in his and dramatically dropped onto his knees. "Will you be my date to the Teen Tube Awards tomorrow night?"

Ruthie couldn't believe it. Was he serious? "Don't you have a date?"

"It was Roxanne. She dumped me."

"Well . . . ," Ruthie stumbled. "I don't have a dress."

Josh grabbed Ruthie's hand and swung open the trailer door. He pulled her onto the back of the golf cart and shouted out at the production assistant. "Take us to the wardrobe department!"

Ruthie glared at him.

"Please," Josh amended. And they were off!

EIGHT

Seconds later, the golf cart swerved around a sharp bend in the road. A giant old building appeared before them. It had only one door, which sat at the landing of a steep set of stairs. The place had a dark, mysterious air about it. Above the door, an ancient sign read:

COSTUME DEPARTMENT

Josh thanked the P.A. for the ride, then grabbed Ruthie's hand and tore up the stairs. As he opened the rickety door, it creaked like a witch's rocking chair. The sunlight from outside spilled into the dark room. Ruthie narrowed her eyes, trying to see past the small ray of light. The room appeared to go on forever.

Josh stepped inside and Ruthie followed, keenly aware of how musty and damp the place smelled. It was like an old attic, only much bigger. As the door creaked shut behind them, Ruthie almost panicked. She grabbed Josh's hand as the light disappeared.

From far away, deep in the belly of the room, Ruthie heard an old lady croak, "Who's there?"

Footsteps creaked toward them along the floor. Josh bellowed out toward the sound.

"Carlotta! It's me, Josh!"

As Ruthie's eyes began adjusting to the dark, she saw that there were rows and rows of hanging costumes filling the room. An old woman in a long black gown emerged from the aisle before them. Her dark hair was pulled up in a messy bun and held there by several long wooden sticks. The gown looked tattered and worn, as if she'd been wearing it for years.

Ruthie took a deep breath when she saw the woman's face: it was ghostly white, though her lips were bright red. To Ruthie's surprise, Josh threw his arm around the woman's shoulder. But she didn't react to the gesture.

"Carlotta, this is Ruthie. Ruthie, this is the crankiest old lady on the lot. She's the only person who's got the guts to be mean to me!"

The woman didn't look up. She was staring at the Victorian gown that was draped across her arm. She had a needle in one hand and a thimble on the other. "What do you want!" she croaked.

"Carlotta," Josh said calmly. "Ruthie is my date to an awards show—"

"What awards show? I don't know of any awards show!"

"The Teen Tube Awards."

"Pshaw! Awards shows for teenagers! Next that Rocket dog of yours will have his own awards show!"

"I know, I know. But it's happening tomorrow night. She needs a gown to wear."

Carlotta pulled a pen out from behind her ear and grabbed a notepad from off the nearest stool. She shoved it in Ruthie's face, still inspecting the gown. "Pick it out and write it down. I'll charge the cleaning fees to production."

As quickly as she had come, Carlotta disappeared into the darkness.

Josh picked up a flashlight from off the stool and turned it on. "Come on," he whispered, and began walking down the aisles. As he pointed the flashlight at different gowns, he explained that every costume in the room had been worn in one of the studio's TV shows or movies.

"You know the screen star Elizabeth Taylor?"

Ruthie nodded, "I've heard of her."

"Heard of her!" Josh exclaimed. "She's a legend!" He held up a green silk gown. "She wore this. You can still smell her perfume."

As Ruthie bent down to smell the dress, Josh pulled her down to another row and reached for a black and white pinstriped suit sealed in a clear garment bag. "Marlene Dietrich," he said, his eyes dancing.

"Who's she?"

Josh smiled. "An even bigger legend than Elizabeth Taylor. She was a German film star who made it big in America, in the '30s and '40s. This was a famous suit that she wore."

Ruthie smiled at Josh. Even though the rest of the day had been difficult, at this moment it was clear how much he loved his job. She could see that Hollywood was still magical for him, just as it had always been for her.

Suddenly something caught her eye. A blue velvet gown. She reached out for it, certain that it would be too large for her to wear.

Josh nodded as she pulled it out of its protective covering. "That gown was worn by Jodie Foster when she was your age."

Ruthie couldn't believe it. "You mean Jodie Foster, the movie star, was a child actress?"

Josh nodded and held the dress up to Ruthie. "Just like me."

The two looked the gown up and down, then looked at each other and smiled. It was exactly her size!

On the drive back to the hotel, Mrs. Camden was very unhappy.

"The Teen Tube Awards, Ruthie? You can't be serious!"

Ruthie couldn't believe her mother would even consider standing in her way.

This was the opportunity of a lifetime! "You can't seriously object!"

"Oh, but I can. Have you forgotten what kind of a boy Josh Kindle is?"

"He's a good person when you get to know him."

"He shut down an entire television show just because he felt like it! Those are people's jobs, Ruthie, their livelihoods. Those people have children to feed and clothe! He's a spoiled-rotten brat."

Ruthie started to object, but Mrs. Camden put her hand up.

"Not only that, he's fifteen."

"Barely!"

"And you're not even thirteen."

"Almost!"

"I don't trust him one bit."

Ruthie rolled her eyes. "Please. I have him wrapped around my little finger."

Mrs. Camden looked down her nose at her daughter. "You're a minnow swimming with sharks, Ruthie. And I don't have an invitation to chaperone."

Just then, Richard's cell phone rang. He answered, then handed it to Mrs. Camden.

"It's Edgar."

Surprised, Mrs. Camden took the phone. "Hello?"

She heard Edgar's mannered voice on the line. "I'm so sorry to call so unexpectedly, but I have a bit of an emergency on my hands."

Mrs. Camden sat up, concerned. "Oh, dear. What can I do?"

Edgar chuckled. "I suppose 'emergency' is too strong of a word. It's just that my wife has fallen ill. . . ."

"Yes . . . ?" Mrs. Camden waited.

"And my daughter is studying for a big test up at Stanford and can't get away for the night."

Mrs. Camden wasn't sure what Edgar was getting at. "For what night?"

"The awards show," Edgar explained. "I need a date—one that my wife would approve of. You're a minister's wife, and the contest winner's mother. She thinks you're the perfect replacement."

Mrs. Camden's jaw actually dropped open in shock. "I'd love to."

"Have Richard bring you to the house. My wife is about your size, and she'd love to loan you a dress."

In that one split second, all of Mrs.

Camden's objections to Ruthie attending the awards show vanished. Mrs. Camden beamed as she hung up the phone, imagining herself on the arm of a big-time producer at a fancy awards show. How could she pass up such an event? And then she understood how Ruthie must have felt.

She smiled down at her daughter and ran her fingers through Ruthie's hair. Sometimes, Mrs. Camden realized, she could be a real stick in the mud. "All right, all right. Permission granted."

Ruthie looked up, amazed at her luck. Had God just worked a miracle for her? Really, what were the chances that her mother would get her own invite to the awards show? Maybe Ruthie really was meant to meet Josh—and maybe not for her sake, but for his?

NINE

The freeways were filled with limousines. Nothing but long black limousines as far as the eye could see. Traffic was at a standstill as the drivers all tried to make their way off the same exit. Ruthie, in her velvet gown, was mesmerized.

Imagine all those stars, hidden behind dark glass windows. And here I am, Ruthie Camden, sitting in the middle of it all. Sitting here with Josh Kindle . . .

She looked at Josh and blushed when she realized he had been looking at her. He had that amazing sparkle in his eye.

"What?" she asked, suddenly shy.

He reached over to take her hand. Just as Josh's hand touched hers, Richard cleared his throat. His eyes were watching them from the rearview mirror.

"Ruthie's mother would like me to remind you that Ruthie is not quite thirteen."

Josh sat upright, embarrassed. "I . . . I just want to hold her hand, I promise."

Richard turned around and looked Josh in the eye. Josh swallowed hard and removed his hand.

"Oh, come on, Richard!" Ruthie exclaimed. "It's okay if we hold hands!" Ruthie grabbed back Josh's hand and smiled at him.

As the limo made its way off the exit and onto the boulevard, Ruthie looked out at all the limousines. Inside one of them, her mother was sitting with Edgar, looking beautiful in her cream-colored gown. Ruthie was proud that Edgar had recognized what an amazing, unique woman her mother was. As she thought about all the wise advice her mother had given her on this trip, it was suddenly clear to Ruthie that her mother *deserved* to be treated like royalty once in a while. Why had Ruthie been such a pain to her before?

As the limo slowed to a stop, Ruthie

looked up at the grand theater before them. The Shrine Auditorium had hosted more awards shows than any other building in Los Angeles. And Ruthie was climbing out of a limousine just like she'd watched the stars do for years!

As Ruthie and Josh stepped out onto the red carpet, cameras flashed all around them. She could feel thousands of eyes on her, staring out from the fan-filled risers that were set up outside the cordoned ropes. But all she could think about was Josh. Once inside the building, he led Ruthie up to a group of teenagers in the lobby and introduced her to each of them. Ruthie recognized over half the faces from different television shows, and was amazed that the young actors greeted her just as any other kids would.

Ruthie looked around the lobby, where clusters of teens in formal attire congregated. She smiled. It was no different than at her school. There were cliques, and even wallflowers—actors who were too shy to talk to anyone and so stood along the wall, alone.

Ruthie felt a hand on her shoulder. She turned around and saw her mother standing beside her in a gorgeous gown. Mrs. Camden smiled, and Ruthie could tell that she was refraining from hugging Ruthie, thinking it would embarrass her. But Ruthie was proud to have Mrs. Camden as her mom. She threw her arms around her mother and whispered in her ear.

"I'm sorry for being such a pain. Thanks for letting me come."

Mrs. Camden pulled back and kissed her daughter's forehead. "I'm amazed at what a beautiful young woman you're becoming, Ruthie. And so proud."

Just then, Edgar approached in his dapper tuxedo. He hesitated for a moment, the tension between him and Josh palpable. Then he put his arm around the young man. "You doing okay, kid?"

Josh took a deep breath and then mustered up a smile. "I am. . . ." He struggled to say what he knew he needed to say. "I'm . . . sorry I walked out yesterday. It was pretty childish of me. I'll be in bright and early Monday."

Edgar couldn't mask his surprise. He smiled, then his face grew serious. "I'm sorry I haven't been there for you, Josh," he said quietly. "I know you've had a tough time with your parents, and I want you to know my door is always open. If you need to talk."

Josh's eyes softened. Ruthie could tell he was touched. She squeezed his hand and he squeezed back.

Suddenly the lights blinked, signaling that the show was about to begin. Josh put his arm around Ruthie. "We better find our seats."

He led her into the auditorium. Once inside, Ruthie's eyes widened. It was like they were entering a palace. A giant crystal chandelier hung from the center of the ceiling, and the architecture was unlike any she had ever seen except in books.

Josh whispered as he led her down front. "We've got the most nominations this season, so we're front and center."

Josh stopped at the second row and Ruthie recognized all of the people from *Too Cool*, who were all seated together. As Ruthie was ushered into her seat, she realized that Roxanne was sitting next to her. For a moment, Ruthie felt awkward—the last time she'd seen Roxanne, she'd been telling Josh off; now here she was on his arm.

But Roxanne's smile wiped all her worries away. "He needs a friend," Roxanne said. "I gave up—but I'm glad you didn't."

Ruthie smiled and thanked Roxanne for being so cool about the whole situation. Then she looked at her program and was astonished at how many awards were being given out. "And that doesn't include all the breaks we have to take for commercials," Josh whispered.

"Where's your category?" Ruthie asked.

Josh pointed to the very end of the page. He was nominated for the very last award of the night.

Just then, a famous comedian walked out onto the stage and the audience began clapping. Ruthie settled into her seat, a huge smile on her face. The show was about to begin!

Four hours later, the awards show was still going strong—and Ruthie had to go to the bathroom. She looked down at her program. There were four awards left to give before Josh's category, as well as a pause for a commercial break. Would she have time? She leaned over and whispered to Josh.

"I have to use the lady's room."

Josh laughed when he saw the worried crease in her forehead. "You should be able to make it back in time. It'll be at least fifteen minutes before I'm up."

Ruthie breathed a sigh of relief and started to get up. Roxanne grabbed her hand and whispered to her.

"That line is brutal. You'd better hurry."

Ruthie nodded and rushed out of the auditorium. When she arrived at the women's bathroom, her heart nearly stopped. The line stretched all the way down the hallway. She looked back toward the auditorium door. . . . Maybe she could just hold on until after the show?

A woman a few feet ahead saw her look and smiled. "It's moving quickly," she said. Ruthie nodded, thinking she recognized the woman. But from where?

Several minutes later, Ruthie had made it inside the bathroom. She was more than halfway through the line, and her bladder was about to burst. Even if she wanted to turn around now, she couldn't. She could barely stand, let alone walk.

That's when she heard the loudspeaker in the bathroom. She could hear the emcee talking to the crowd. The commercial break was over, and there was only one award left to give before Josh's! How could she possibly make it back?

The woman who had spoken to her before was now at the front of the line. Just as a stall door opened, the woman turned around and looked at Ruthie. That's when Ruthie realized who the woman was. She had been holding the boom microphone on the *Too Cool* set.

The woman laughed when she saw Ruthie's exasperated expression. "Switch places with me," she said. "I don't need to see Josh get another award."

Ruthie squealed out of pure joy and ran toward the open stall door. "I owe you one!" Ruthie exclaimed.

"No, we owe you one," the woman replied.

When Ruthie was finished at the sink, she ran up to the woman and gave her a big hug, then fled out of the bathroom. As she flung open the auditorium door, an usher stopped her.

"It's the middle of a speech," the man said. "You can't walk to your seat until it's over."

Ruthie looked down at the stage and

had to hold in another squeal. Josh was standing on the stage!

"Did he win Hottest Hunk?" she whispered.

The usher nodded and held his finger to his lips to shush her. Then Josh took the microphone.

"Normally I'd act like my fly self right now and, you know, strut around the stage, because that's who I am, right?" He puffed up his chest and swaggered about as he talked.

The audience laughed. There were whistles and catcalls coming from up in the balcony. Grinning, Josh waited for all the noise to subside. Then he got serious and looked out at the audience.

"But yesterday I met a girl who made me realize how pompous I can really be. And that there are more important things in life than being cool or being a star." He looked in the second row, disappointed when he saw that Ruthie wasn't in her seat. "Of course, she's stuck in the bathroom right now. . . ."

The audience laughed again as they watched him comb the auditorium with his eyes, looking for her. Shyly, Ruthie held up a hand. And then the usher began waving his arms and pointing at her.

Josh spotted her and laughed. "No, wait, there she is!" He pointed and suddenly all the cameras that were placed around the auditorium swung around toward her. Embarrassed, Ruthie smiled, staring up at Josh.

"So I dedicate this award to Ruthie Camden," he said. "For bringing me back down to Earth."

TEN

Back in the sleepy town of Glenoak, the entire neighborhood was gathered on the Camdens' front lawn. On the front page of the morning *Glenoak News* was a picture of Ruthie holding Josh's hand. The headline read:

SMALL-TOWN GIRL MAKES IT BIG!

Blocks away, Ruthie and Mrs. Camden were in the backseat of Richard's limousine. Ruthie was cramming for her social studies exam, but it was hard—Mrs. Camden wouldn't stop talking about the awards ceremony.

"It was just delightful, Richard!" she exclaimed. "All those gorgeous gowns, and the jewelry, and the lights, and the stars . . ."

"Why, Mrs. Camden," Richard began. "I do believe you're starstruck."

"Starstruck?" Mrs. Camden exclaimed. "Me? I'm not starstruck! No, it's not about the stars. It's about the magic of Hollywood."

Ruthie rolled her eyes. "The magic of Hollywood? Somebody wasn't listening to her own lecture."

Mrs. Camden laughed and squeezed her daughter's leg. "I admit it: I was a bit judgmental when I first arrived. But I can't deny it any longer. There is magic in Hollywood. There's also greed and deceit, but magic, too. And last night was a truly magical night."

As they turned onto their street, Mrs. Camden pulled the remaining cash out of her pocket. There was plenty left of the tip money she had been given.

"Richard," she said, leaning over the seat. "I want to thank you for driving us home. I just couldn't handle another propeller plane." She dropped the cash on the seat next to him.

As Richard began to protest, the car slowed to a stop in front of the Camdens' house. And instead of waiting for him to open her door, Mrs. Camden flung the door open and stepped out. Before she had time to realize what was happening in the front yard, she felt two giant arms embrace her.

Her husband, Reverend Camden, whispered in her ear. "No Hollywood producer can outdazzle my wife!" He swooped her up in his arms, dipped her like a classic movie star, and planted a big kiss on her lips. The neighbors went wild as their cameras flashed.

Then Ruthie said goodbye to Richard, thanked him, and reached for her sunglasses. If the neighbors wanted a Hollywood show, she'd be happy to give it to them! She slid the glasses on and stepped out dramatically.

As the cameras flashed, Ruthie struck pose after pose. Just as she was about to bow, she saw her sister Mary running through the crowd toward her.

"Uh-oh," Ruthie said. Mary had that look in her eye. Ruthie threw off her glasses and took off running. But before she could get anywhere, Mary tackled her—and the rest of the Camden siblings attacked en masse.

"Remember how Josh thanked you for bringing him back down to Earth?" Mary grinned, her hands attacking Ruthie's stomach.

Ruthie screamed, laughing. "Stop! That tickles!"

"Well, that's what you'll be thanking us for for the rest of your life!" Mary shouted.

As she tried to catch her breath from laughing too hard, Ruthie looked up at all the loving faces of her friends and family—and then she thought of Josh, sitting all alone in his trailer, running through the costume department with Carlotta, driving through the city in limousines. . . .

Hollywood was great, no question. But if this was what being on Earth was all about—being surrounded by brothers and sisters who love you, by neighbors who care, by parents who work so hard to do the right thing—who could ask for anything more?

THE BEST
OKTOBERFEST

ONE

Robbie tossed his books into the corner and peeled off his jacket. He draped it over the rack and headed for the refrigerator. Ruthie smiled at him from her chair at the kitchen table. She clutched a bundle of mail in her hand. She was done with her exams and ready for her next adventure.

"Can't you just feel that brisk autumn chill?" she cooed. "Don't you smell a sharp touch of frost in the air? Doesn't the promise of winter make your blood tingle?"

Robbie raised an eyebrow. "Ruthie, it's seventy degrees outside. And, to be honest, I *don't* feel the creeping sensation of that first frigid stroke of winter's imminent embrace—not here in sunny Glenoak, anyway."

Ruthie's eyes went wide. "Nice vocabulary! You *are* learning a thing or two at that school."

Opening the refrigerator, Robbie winked. "Wait till you see my grades."

"Okay," Ruthie said, returning to her original subject. "Maybe you *don't* feel the promise of winter, but wouldn't you *like* to? Wouldn't you like to fill your lungs with crisp mountain air?"

"I'd *like* to find the baloney."

"Too late." Ruthie grinned. "Simon beat you to it."

Robbie closed the refrigerator and poured two glasses of milk. "When did Simon get home?"

"A couple of minutes ago," Ruthie said. "But he didn't stick around very long, not after I handed him his invitation."

"Invitation? Invitation to what?"

"Here's yours. Read it for yourself." Ruthie took the cold glass of milk and handed Robbie an envelope in return.

Robbie set his glass down on the table, opened the envelope, and scanned its contents.

"Hey! This sounds pretty cool."

Ruthie smiled from ear to ear. "Read about the Big/Little Games. That's the best part!"

Just then, Simon entered with an empty glass in one hand and an empty plate in the other. He absentmindedly dumped them in the sink before he even noticed Robbie holding his invitation.

"Hey, Simon! Did you see—"

"Don't say another word!" Simon cried. "No matter what you say, no matter what anyone says, I am not going to Oktoberfest!"

Robbie blinked, baffled. "What's wrong with Oktoberfest?"

"Nothing!" Simon yelled as he raced up the stairs.

Robbie turned to Ruthie for answers. "What's *that* about?"

She shook her head, put her finger to her lips, then whispered, "The Doubler twins."

"The Doubler twins?" Robbie demanded. "What are they?"

Ruthie instantly shushed him. "Not so loud!" she hissed. "They're a *who*, not a what—and we don't talk about them around here because Simon has never recovered from the embarrassment."

Robbie sat down across the table from Ruthie and looked the girl in the eye. "Talk to me," he said. "What's really going on here?"

Ruthie's eyes scanned the doorway to make sure they were alone, then she leaned over the table to whisper close to Robbie's ear.

"Two years ago, Matt and Simon were utterly and completely humiliated by the Doubler twins—two supermen who go to Reverend Gerst's church."

"The Doubler twins are *guys*?" Robbie asked, still confused.

"Big guys!" she replied, indicating their massive size with a wave of her arms. "They were so big I think they were shaving in third grade! And the Doubler twins could do things that Matt and Simon couldn't. Not in a million years!"

"Like what?"

Ruthie began ticking off the list on her fingers. "Sack racing. Apple bobbing. Horseshoes. Tug-of-war. Frisbee tossing. Spoon races. Treasure hunting. Hoops. That weird game where you hit a piece of wood with a big mallet and the metal thingie goes up the rail and rings the bell—"

"The Doubler twins beat Matt and Simon at *that*?"

"Actually, *Mary* beat Matt and Simon at that one," Ruthie confessed. "But, believe me, losing to Mary didn't make their Oktoberfest any better!"

"What did Reverend Camden say when all this happened?"

"Mom and Dad don't know about it," Ruthie replied. "They never go to Oktoberfest, except when they volunteer for the chaperone committee, and they haven't done that since Sam and David were born."

"Wait a minute," Robbie said. "All this happened a couple of years ago, right? How do we even know the Doubler twins will show up this time?"

Ruthie waved the schedule under his nose. "It says right here, in the list of Reverend Gerst's church attendees—'E. and G. Doubler.' Evan and Gerhart. . . . It's got to be them. How many Doubler twins could there be in the world?"

"Did Simon see this list?"

Ruthie crossed her arms. "What do *you* think?"

"This is terrible!" Robbie moaned.

"It's not *that* bad," Ruthie replied. "Mary and Lucy are going. And we can all have plenty of fun, even *without* Simon."

She leaned across the table and pointed at the schedule of events.

"For instance, you and I can sign up for the Big/Little Games. That's where a little brother or sister can win really cool prizes by teaming up with his or her big brother or sister.

"I know you're not really my brother, but since you live here I'm sure the judges will overlook that minor technicality—"

Just then Mary and Lucy burst into the kitchen. Before he even had a chance to take a sip, Mary seized Robbie's glass of milk and downed it in three big gulps.

"Thanks. I was thirsty," she said, wiping her mouth with Robbie's napkin.

"Oh, wow!" Lucy cried. "The Oktoberfest invitations have arrived."

Mary's eyes twinkled mischievously. "I wonder if Simon got *his* invitation."

"That's really mean," Lucy said with a giggle. Mary tried to keep a straight face, but couldn't.

"Like he's even going to go!" she laughed.

"Hey! What makes you so sure Simon's not going to Oktoberfest?" Robbie asked peevishly.

Lucy grinned. "Did you talk him into it?"

Robbie turned away. "Not . . . yet."

"Well," Mary said, flexing her biceps. "If you *do* manage to convince Simon to come with us, tell him he'd better stay away from that 'ring the bell' game if he knows what's good for him."

She and Lucy both chuckled as they headed upstairs.

"This is bad," Robbie sighed. "I can't let Simon take this abuse any longer. He needs a big brother to watch out for him . . . help him beat those Doubler twins and restore his manly honor once and for all!"

"He's already *got* a big brother," Ruthie replied. "And, frankly, Matt wasn't much help in the 'manly honor' department."

"Matt wants me to watch out for Simon. He even said so," cried Robbie. "Remember that talk he gave me before he went off to medical school?"

It was Ruthie's turn to moan. "Oh, yeah," she said, rolling her eyes. "The *talk*."

"Matt asked me to watch out for Simon, try to be Simon's big brother while he's away."

Ruthie just shook her head.

"Listen, Robbie! You've got to let it go. Matt's given me plenty of talks over the years. I forgot most of them and ignored the rest. What's important here is the relationship between you and me, right? Why have a miserable time with Simon when you can have fun with me?"

"This is important," Robbie insisted. "Simon needs to get his self-respect back, and I have a duty to help."

"What about *my* self-respect?" Ruthie cried. "It will plummet if I don't compete! Every Oktoberfest is the same. Matt and Simon team up; Mary and Lucy team up. I'm always sitting in the bleachers, watching. This year I want to be out there on the field, winning the glory—and those Big/Little Game prizes!"

But Robbie wasn't listening anymore.

"I have a responsibility to make this right," he said. "It's what Matt would want me to do."

Suddenly Robbie leaped out of his chair. "Simon *can't* give up. He has to face these Doubler guys again, or he'll run away from his problems for the rest of his life."

"Wait!" Ruthie cried. "What about me!"

"Come on, Ruthie. You have a real sister—two of them. You can always team up with Mary . . . or even Lucy."

"Yeah, Lucy would be great," Ruthie sighed. "If the prizes were awarded for best klutz."

"We'll talk later," said Robbie. "Right now, I need to discuss this situation with Simon!"

TWO

"Wouldn't you love to get back at those guys?" Robbie asked for the fifth time.

Simon shrugged. "Sure, but how am I going to do that?"

"With *me* as your big brother," Robbie said, thrusting his thumb in his chest.

"Forget it," said Simon. "I already have a big brother, and sometimes—like *now*—even one feels like too many."

"Come on!" Robbie poked Simon's arm. "Where's your sporting blood?"

"In my *veins*, where I like it," Simon shot back. "Those Doubler twins are really tough, and really bad winners. They taunted Matt and me every time we lost—in front of everybody!"

Simon's brow furrowed at the memory. "Not only did they kill us, they also made us feel about two inches tall!"

"So they're lousy sports," Robbie said. "All the more reason to get back at them."

"I don't think so," Simon said with an uncertain frown. "Anyway, that was years ago."

"And revenge is a dish best served cold."

Simon stared at Robbie until the older boy blinked. "I heard that in a *Star Trek* movie," Robbie confessed sheepishly.

"Well, if quoting *Star Trek* is the best you can come up with, forget it," Simon said as he opened a book. Robbie lingered, wondering what to say to convince Simon.

"I have to do my homework now," Simon told him. "So run along."

As Robbie closed the door behind him, he met Ruthie in the hall.

"You've been in and out of Simon's room all afternoon," she said. "Why don't you give up and face the facts? You and me—we're destined to be together."

Robbie shook his head. "It's not over until it's over," he announced stubbornly.

"It looks like it's over to me."

"Well, I haven't given up," Robbie said. Then he smiled, remembering he had a secret weapon—two of them, actually—courtesy of Reverend Camden.

"Just admit it. Even if you do compete in the Oktoberfest games, you and Simon don't have a chance," said Ruthie. "But you and I, on the other hand, can win easily. And there's not much chance you'll get injured in the Big/Little Games."

"Who said I'll get injured in *any* games?"

"All I know is that those Doubler twins probably eat little guys like you and Simon for breakfast."

"Little?" Robbie said defensively. "Who's little?"

"Not you," Ruthie replied with a sly smile. "Not for the Big/Little Games, anyway."

Ruthie waved the Oktoberfest schedule under Robbie's nose.

"This is your last chance. Team up with me before I go to Mary or Lucy. You don't want to end up without a partner."

Robbie glanced at his watch, wondering when his "secret weapons" would arrive. Just then the doorbell rang.

"Here they are!" Robbie cried.

"Who?" Ruthie demanded, following Robbie down to the front door. She had a tough time keeping up—he was in a hurry, and taking the stairs two at a time.

"My secret weapons," he called over his shoulder.

"Is that what you were on the telephone talking to Dad about?" Ruthie demanded. "You were whispering for an awfully long time."

Robbie shushed her as the doorbell rang a second time.

"Yes, Reverend Camden and I *were* talking about Oktoberfest. And about Simon," he confessed. "But not so loud! I don't want Simon to know."

"You don't want Simon to know *what*?" Ruthie said loudly. "That you and Dad were plotting behind his back?"

Robbie shushed her again. When the doorbell rang a third time, Mary appeared at the top of the steps.

"Isn't anybody going to answer the door?" she called. Lucy and Simon appeared on the landing behind her. Robbie spotted Simon and smiled.

"I'll get it!" Robbie yelled back.

Robbie straightened his shirt and ran his hands through his hair. As Ruthie, Mary, Lucy, and Simon watched expectantly, Robbie turned the knob and the front door swung open.

"Is this the home of Reverend and Mrs. Camden?"

Robbie was tongue-tied. He just stared, mouth gaping, at the two lovely young women—obviously twins—standing on the front porch.

Vaguely, Robbie noticed Ruthie tugging on his arm. He looked down at her and she beckoned him with her finger. When Robbie bent low, Ruthie placed her hand under his jaw and pushed his mouth closed.

The girls waiting in the doorway giggled.

"Are you Robbie?" one of the twins asked.

"Ah . . . yes," Robbie stammered. "I are . . . I mean, I *am*."

He extended his hand. "You must be Greta and Erika."

The twins nodded as one, their blond hair bobbing, their blue eyes twinkling with amusement.

"I am Greta," said one.

"I am Erika," said the other. Robbie smiled at them both. He was completely charmed.

"Welcome to America!" Robbie said. "Reverend Camden told me you were from Germany."

"*Ja* . . . I mean, yes," Erika replied. "We are staying with our aunt and uncle. They attend Reverend Gerst's church, so we are going to Oktoberfest, like you."

"Yes," Greta said. "I am looking forward to seeing how Americans celebrate Oktoberfest."

Above them, on the landing, Lucy and Mary stared down at the girls. Mary guessed they were younger than Robbie, but older than Simon.

"They sure are . . . tall," Mary whispered. "And blond."

"Yes," Lucy replied. "*Naturally* blond. And . . . fit. Very, very *fit*."

"Excuse me," Simon said as he pushed past Mary and Lucy and bounded down the steps.

"So you are going to help us organize?" Erika asked.

"You bet," said Robbie. "I'll be glad to help out." He glanced at his watch. "Let's go."

A hand seized Robbie's arm. "Not so fast," said Simon. "Aren't you going to introduce me?"

"Of course!" Robbie said. "I forgot my manners."

"Like you forgot to close your *mouth*," Ruthie said. Then she walked away in disgust.

"So what are you guys doing?" Simon asked after introductions were over.

"Greta and Erika are going to Oktoberfest," Robbie said. "I'm helping with the organizing committee."

"What a coincidence!" Simon cried. "I'm going to Oktoberfest, too. I'm going to be Robbie's partner in the games."

When she heard those words, Ruthie's eyes widened in surprise. So did Mary's and Lucy's.

"Maybe I can help out with the committee, too?" Simon said hopefully.

"Don't you have homework to do?" Robbie asked. Simon shrugged.

Erika turned to Simon. "We wouldn't want you to neglect your schoolwork," she said. "But it was very nice to meet you."

"Very nice," Greta added, her smile warm.

"Really!" Simon said, staring at Greta. "It's no trouble. I'd be glad to help. . . ."

Robbie stepped between Simon and the girls. "It's under control," he said.

"Goodbye, Simon," said Greta sweetly. "I hope to see you at Oktoberfest!"

"Me too!" Simon said. "That is, I hope to see you there as well."

"Gotta go," Robbie announced, pushing the girls along.

"Goodbye!" Simon called after them as Robbie and the twins drove away.

Unseen by anyone, Ruthie slumped down on the living room couch. Frowning, she stared at the floor.

"Not only did I lose my only chance at competing in the Big/Little Games, I lost Robbie to those German girls, too."

Happy waddled over to Ruthie and sat down. The dog gazed up with big, dark eyes as Ruthie stroked her head.

"Okay, Robbie, go ahead and partner with Simon! But if you think you're going to get a new German girlfriend out of this Oktoberfest mess, then you've got another thing coming!"

THREE

"Smell that fresh mountain air!" Robbie said as he climbed out of the car. To emphasize the point he took a deep breath, then pounded his chest.

"It's great!"

"Well, the traffic wasn't bad, for a Friday," Simon said, stretching muscles made stiff from the long drive. He scanned the parking lot. It was already filling up.

"Looks like we beat my sisters here," Simon observed.

"That's because Lucy was driving," Robbie said as he opened the trunk and handed Simon his gym bag.

"That's all you packed?"

Simon shrugged. "How much do we

need? It's only two nights in the mountains—not a dress formal." He began walking toward a gate with a big OKTOBERFEST sign over it.

"These mountains are really something," Robbie said, gazing at a line of peaks in the distance. A chill wind kicked up just then, causing him to shiver. Robbie zipped up his jacket.

"I wonder where our tent is?" Simon said.

"Tent?" Robbie cried. "We're staying in a *tent*?"

Simon grinned. "What, didn't you read the brochure? Did you think we'd be staying in a four-star hotel?"

Robbie shook his head. "No, but I was hoping for a log cabin, at least."

"We get a tent and a couple of cots," Simon replied. "We *are* in the middle of the woods here, so we're going to have to rough it."

Robbie frowned.

"I guess I never thought of that," he said. "I figured since we were staying in a national park, we'd stay in a ski lodge or something. A place with a real roof over our heads."

"What's wrong with a tent?" Simon asked. "You lived on the streets of Glenoak for a couple of weeks; why get squeamish about sleeping in a tent?"

Robbie shrugged. "I guess I'm just a city kid at heart. The country makes me nervous."

Overhead, a high-flying hawk cried out. Robbie jumped, startled.

Simon chuckled. "Some big brother *you* are."

Leaves blew across their path and the breeze stirred the branches of the tall pines as Robbie and Simon entered the gate. The late-afternoon air was crisp and clean, and hinted of cooler air to come. Inside the compound, Robbie spotted lines of tents in the distance. Simon tapped his arm and pointed in the direction of the registration table.

After they signed in and got their tent number, Simon and Robbie proceeded to the events calendar posted on a large wooden bulletin board.

"Here's the list of activities, and there are the competitions," Simon announced. Then he turned to examine the crowds of teenagers still filing into the campground.

"I wonder if Greta and Erika are here yet?"

"Forget about them," said Robbie as he scanned the competition list. "We're here to get one over on the Doubler twins, remember?"

Simon rolled his eyes.

"Horseshoes, sack races, spoon races, Frisbee tossing—it doesn't sound too bad," Robbie observed. "And men and women compete together—so that's a plus. Half the competition will be easy to beat."

Simon smiled as he watched two young girls saunter by. They were both skinny, and had braces. They struggled under the weight of their small bags. "You're right," Simon announced. "How hard can it be to beat girls?"

Robbie turned and high-fived Simon. Then they both laughed.

"I know we can do this!" Robbie said, brimming with confidence.

For a moment, Simon fell for Robbie's pep talk. Then he frowned, pointing to one name that repeatedly appeared on the competition list.

"The Doubler twins have signed up for

just about every event," he noted.

Robbie lifted a pencil that dangled on the end of a string. "Then so will we."

Simon watched with mounting apprehension as Robbie signed them up for a dozen events. Suddenly Robbie paused as he read the brief description of one particular competition.

"What's this treasure hunt all about?" Robbie asked.

"The judges give two-people teams a compass and a map and send them into the woods to hunt for some kind of 'treasure.' The winner is the first person to bring the treasure back to camp."

Robbie got a little pale. "So we actually go into the wilderness . . . by ourselves?"

"Well, we won't be *completely* alone," Simon replied with a smirk. "Don't forget . . . these mountains *are* full of bears."

Robbie dropped the pencil, letting it swing from the string. He hesitated, then lifted it again and placed the lead tip on the line. Simon opened his mouth to speak, but, before he could say a word, Robbie quickly added his and Simon's names to the treasure hunt list.

"Let's go find our tent," Robbie said, grabbing his bag and hurrying toward the tents.

Before I change my mind . . .

"That drive took, like, *forever*!" Mary cried in exasperation. Ruthie nodded in agreement.

Lucy opened the door and climbed out of the van. "If you thought I was driving too slowly, then you should have driven here by yourself!"

"I *know* you were driving too slowly, but I couldn't get here on my own because my car's in the shop," Mary shot back.

"Not to worry," she added with false sweetness. "On Sunday, when we go home, it's *my* turn to drive!"

Lucy shook her head. "I am *so* looking forward to becoming a traffic statistic."

Instead of replying, Mary popped open the van's rear hatch and began tossing out bags. A frigid wind off the mountains made Mary shiver. "It's cold!"

"I told you not to wear those shorts," Lucy replied. "They don't look like they're very warm. . . ."

Mary's eyes twinkled. "They're not supposed to be warm—they are supposed to be *attractive*. I don't know about you, but I'm here to have fun, and meeting guys is at the top of my agenda!"

Lucy rolled her eyes.

"Hey, what's in here?" Mary asked, pulling a pink Powerpuff Girls backpack out of the back of the van.

"That's mine!" Ruthie cried, reaching out to grab it. Lucy pulled the bag away, then peered at the contents jammed inside.

"There sure is a lot of bubble gum and lip balm in here," Lucy marveled. Ruthie gripped the handle and yanked the bag out of her sister's hand.

"Hey!"

"There's a lot of other stuff in here besides bubble gum and lip balm," Ruthie explained, hugging the pink sack close. "I've got survival stuff. Like Band-Aids, cotton balls, sun block, a hook and some fishing line, a compass—"

"And a pink refrigerator magnet," Lucy said, dangling a little plastic bunny in front of Mary.

In one swift motion, Ruthie snatched the tiny magnet from Lucy's hand and thrust it deep inside her plastic sack.

"What's the little mirror for?" Lucy said. "Cosmetic emergencies?"

Ruthie fished the mirror out of the bag, held it up, and twisted it in her hand until it caught the sunlight

"If I get lost in the forest, I can signal passing airplanes for help," Ruthie declared. "And I brought the fishing stuff in case we have to live off the land."

Mary crossed her arms and stared suspiciously at her little sister. "What do you *really* need all that stuff for?"

Ruthie opened her arms to indicate their surroundings. "Look where we are!" she cried. "In the middle of the woods, with owls and bears and foxes and who-knows-what else? And we're going to spend the next two nights in a *tent*!"

Ruthie nodded sagely. "Under these conditions, I figure a girl can't have too much bubble gum or lip balm."

"Wait a minute," Lucy said, hands on her hips. "Are we talking to Ruthie Camden, resident outdoorswoman and future champion equestrian?"

"My knowledge of the outdoors only gives me a greater appreciation of the potential hazards we might face," said Ruthie.

"Whatever," Mary said, gathering up her stuff. "Let's go register and find our tent."

After the girls checked in, Ruthie ran over to the events calendar posted on the bulletin board. She scanned it and stamped her foot angrily.

"What's the matter?" Mary asked.

"Lucy drove so slowly that we missed the first Big/Little Game—the Frisbee toss," Ruthie complained.

"So what?" cried Lucy. "You're not competing! You absolutely refused to let Mary or me team up with you."

"Frankly, I was hoping for a better partner," Ruthie said with a frown.

"Thanks a lot!" Lucy turned and walked back to Mary.

"Face it," Ruthie called after her. "You are as slow at sack racing as you are at driving—what chance did we really have?"

"You had a great chance of winning with me as your partner," Mary said. "But you held out for Robbie, and now Robbie has teamed up with Simon."

Ruthie frowned, but said nothing.

"Now it's too late, because I don't want to team up with you. I am here to have fun," Mary declared as she scanned her brochure. "And the Saturday night hayride sounds like fun to me."

"You mean it sounds like a good place to meet boys," Ruthie shot back.

Lucy clapped her hands. Let's get tickets now!"

At the events table, a volunteer from Reverend Gerst's church smiled up at them. "You two young ladies are lucky," the woman explained. "These are the last two tickets for the hayride—it's always a very popular event."

"Thanks!" Mary said.

"Fun, fun, fun!" Lucy exclaimed.

Together, the Camden sisters went on a quest to find their tent.

"Here we are!" Lucy declared. "Number 92." She pushed the flap aside and entered, Mary and Ruthie following behind. There were three cots in the tent, and a light dangling from a cord near the center tent pole.

"Nice accommodations," Lucy remarked sarcastically.

"These tents are smaller than I remember them. But hey, we're here to rough it," Mary said.

Lucy and Mary deposited their bags next to their cots.

"Let's look around," Lucy said. "See what's happening."

Mary nodded. "Want to come, Ruthie?"

"No thanks," the girl replied. She sat down on a cot and bounced up and down a couple times. "I think I'm going to unpack my survival stuff and read a good book."

Lucy's jaw dropped. "You're going to read a book?" She shook her head. "That settles it, Ruthie is missing! And she has obviously been replaced by this alien double."

Lucy laughed at her own joke. No one else did.

"Suit yourself," said Mary. "Lucy and I have a better chance of having fun without our little sister tagging along, anyway."

Ruthie frowned again, but turned away before her sisters noticed.

Together, Mary and Lucy took off. When she was finally alone, Ruthie reached into her bag, drew out a book, and began to read. The fading light of the fall afternoon illuminated the bold red title: *The Kids' Guide to Really Cool Practical Jokes.*

FOUR

On Saturday morning, the sun rose bright in the clear blue autumn sky. The alpine air was bracing, and the mountains were an indigo line in the distance, capped by a frosting of pure white snow.

Robbie rose from his cot and stretched his sore and tired muscles. He didn't remember when he'd finally fallen asleep, but he knew it was long after midnight. The uncomfortable cot, and the unaccustomed night sounds of the mountains—wind whistling through the pines, owls hooting, coyotes baying—all combined to rob him of a good night's sleep. But Robbie knew Simon was counting on him—so he had to try to be at his best.

"Wake up call!" one of the program directors announced, his voice booming through the loudspeakers scattered all over camp. The greeting was followed by a recording of a trumpet playing reveille—loudly.

Simon sat up so fast he got twisted up in his blankets and fell off the cot.

"Easy, Simon," Robbie told him. "It's only reveille."

Simon rubbed the sleep out of his eyes. "I had a wonderful dream," he said. "I dreamed I was sleeping—at home, in Glenoak, in my own bed."

"You'll feel better after breakfast," Robbie promised.

After cold scrambled eggs, soggy bacon, and burnt toast, Simon and Robbie headed back to their tent to get ready for the first event.

"It's the sack race," Robbie told Simon, who smiled in relief.

"That doesn't sound too bad," he said.

"No, no," Robbie sighed. "Your attitude is all wrong! You've got to go into these events with fire in your belly."

Simon stifled a belch. "After *that* breakfast, I've got fire in my belly, all right," he moaned.

"Not *that* kind of fire," Robbie said. "I mean that burning need for *victory*. The feeling that you just want to get out there and sweep the competition off the field! The need to play until there's nobody left standing but you!"

"Yeah. *Yeah!*" cried Simon, beginning to get into the spirit.

Robbie clenched his fist and pumped his arm. "When we go out there today, we've got to think like a *team*. Every move we make has to be coordinated. We have to think, move, and react like a two-headed, four-legged, well-oiled machine—a machine that doesn't know the meaning of the word 'defeat'!"

"Right on!" cried Simon.

"Now let's grab our gear and get down to the field!" said Robbie. "And remember—we're a team. An unstoppable victory machine!"

"Got it!" Simon said.

As they swung around to grab their gear, Simon and Robbie collided, their heads clunking together.

"Sorry," Simon said sheepishly.

"My fault," Robbie replied.

As they left the tent with their bags in hand, both Robbie and Simon began to suspect that they might not be an unstoppable victory machine after all.

A shrill whistle blew. "Teams One through Seven—on the line now," the referee commanded.

"Seven! That's us," Robbie said, tugging on Simon's arm.

"Wait until I tie my sneakers!"

Simon hurriedly finished the knot, then ran onto the middle of the field alongside Robbie. Each of them wore a paper sign sporting the number "7" on his back.

The bleachers around the contest area were crowded, but Robbie managed to spot Mary and Lucy in the crowd, and waved to them. Mary and Lucy waved back. Mary even blew them a kiss. On the sidelines at ground level, Ruthie appeared. She was still carrying her pink Powerpuff Girls survival bag.

"Here's your sack, Team Seven," the referee said as he tossed the boys a huge canvas bag. Simon shook out his arms and legs to loosen up.

"Any sign of those Doubler twins?" asked Robbie. Simon stopped stretching and scanned the guys on the line, ignoring the girl teams.

"I don't see them," Simon said, feeling a little relieved.

"Well, they have to be here somewhere," Robbie said. "Their names were on the list."

The whistle blew again. "Okay, teams. Each of you put both feet in the sack and pull it up to waist height," the ref commanded.

Robbie and Simon both got into the sack. In order to move forward, they would have to hop in perfect unison. The top of the bag got tangled on Simon's belt. Ruthie rushed in from the sidelines and helped untangle it.

"Thanks, Ruthie," said Simon.

As Simon and Robbie scanned the crowd, Ruthie drew a fishhook out of her bag. The hook was attached to an almost invisible and incredibly strong fishing line. Unseen, she attached the hook to the bottom of the canvas bag.

"Good luck," Ruthie cried, hurrying away. As the crowd waited for the race to begin, Ruthie discreetly tied the fishing line to a steel fence pole and gently tugged on the string. Then she smiled in triumph.

Tensely, Robbie and Simon waited for the signal to begin the race.

"Hello, Robbie . . . Simon," a voice called from nearby.

Robbie turned, and was shocked to see Greta and Erika on the starting line, just one sack team away. Simon spotted them, too.

"Hey," he said, waving to Greta.

"I didn't know you were in this race," said Robbie.

"Oh, yes," Erika replied, "We are Team Six."

Then the girls waved to a couple sitting in the bleachers.

Robbie noticed them. "Are they your parents?"

"No," Erika said. "Our aunt and uncle. We are visiting them here in America. Our cousins Gerhart and Evan went off to college with a football scholarship, so Greta and I agreed to represent the family at Oktoberfest."

"That's nice," said Simon.

The referee raised his right hand. "On your mark . . ."

"It's more than nice," Greta said as she and her sister got into position. "It is a matter of honor. . . . Everyone in the Doubler family is very competitive."

Simon paled and Robbie's jaw dropped. "You . . . *you're* the Doubler twins?" Simon stammered.

"Get set," the referee shouted.

"Yes," Erika replied with a nod. "Greta and Erika Doubler. Didn't you know our last names?"

"GO!"

Like lightning, Greta and Erika hopped forward, moving down the field toward the finish line. The other teams started moving a split second later. One team stumbled and fell, both teammates laughing as they rolled in the grass.

Robbie and Simon, still in shock, got an awkward start. As Simon shot forward, Robbie nearly lost his balance.

"Let's go!" Simon urged.

Simon and Robbie began to hop as one, moving forward rapidly. Within a moment, they were even with the front-runners—the Doubler twins.

Ruthie watched as the fishing line played out. When the boys were halfway down the track, the string pulled taut.

Simon tried to hop, but it seemed as if the canvas bag had caught on something.

"Move, Camden!"

"I can't!" Simon cried. "The sack is stuck."

Simon hopped again, trying to free himself. Instead, he lost his balance and almost knocked both himself and Robbie to the ground.

"Whoa!" Robbie cried.

Under the bleachers, Ruthie decided to end the competition. She grabbed the fishing line and gave it a hard tug. The hook ripped free of the canvas, but not before it jerked the boys off balance again.

"Look out!" yelled Simon as they both tumbled to the ground, their legs tangled in the sack.

"Great move, Simon!" Robbie complained as he brushed grass out of his hair.

Simon tried to pull his foot out of the sack, but it was stuck. His foot had ripped through the hole Ruthie had made with the fishing hook.

"Hey! I think we got a bum sack," Robbie said with a frown.

"How come you didn't tell me that Greta was a Doubler!" Simon cried.

"Because I didn't know. And anyway, they aren't *the* Doubler twins," Robbie shot back. "They're the Doubler twins' cousins—the *other* Doubler twins."

"And you didn't know that?"

"I swear I didn't," Robbie replied. "But what's the difference? The pressure's off now. No need to beat the girls, because the girls aren't Evan and Gerhart, and they probably aren't bad winners. We can just relax and have fun."

A shadow fell over the two boys. They looked up, squinting into the bright morning sun.

"These American boys are not very competitive, are they, Greta?" Erika taunted.

"They certainly were easy to beat," her sister added with an annoying chuckle.

"Be careful," Erika cautioned as she watched Simon untangle his foot. "You boys might hurt yourselves."

"Okay, Team Six, you're the winners!"

the referee said, rushing up and pointing to the Doubler twins. "Get over to the winner's circle and collect your trophy."

Then the ref stared down at Robbie and Simon. "You two . . . Team Seven, isn't it? Clear the field. And you're lucky I won't have you both disqualified for ruining a perfectly good sack!"

Then the ref stalked off, blowing his whistle and summoning the next teams to the starting line.

"I can't believe this," Simon moaned, tossing the torn bag aside.

"It's not *that* bad, is it?" Robbie said. "Not as bad as losing to their cousins?"

"They're girls," Simon said, burying his face in his hands. "Which makes defeat at their hands so much worse."

As the boys limped back to the benches, the Camden sisters greeted them.

"Tough luck," Lucy said. "But I'm sure you'll do better next time."

"Yeah," said Mary. "The next event is a tug-of-war. How hard can that be?"

"Here's your stuff," Ruthie said. She smiled as she handed Simon and Robbie their gym bags.

FIVE

"Better change into your all-terrain sneakers for the tug-of-war," Ruthie suggested.

"Ruthie's right," Mary added. "You guys are going to need all the traction you can get for this event."

Robbie sat down and changed into his all-terrain track shoes. Simon did the same.

"On the line for the tug-of-war!" the referee cried. "Odd numbers to the right, even numbers to the left."

Everyone ran onto the field and sorted themselves out. Simon slipped in the grass and Robbie eyed him suspiciously.

"What is this, 'clumsy day'?"

"Shut up," Simon shot back.

The ref moved among the teams, sorting them out further until eight people—four teams—were on each rope. Robbie and Simon found themselves teamed up with Team Nine—two petite teenage girls from Reverend Gerst's church, the very girls Simon saw struggling under the weight of their luggage the day before.

On the other side of the rope, two big football players from the Glenoak high school team were paired with the Doubler twins.

Between the two ends of the rope was a patch of brown, sticky mud. The losers of the tug-of-war would end up ankle-deep in muck.

"Oh, no," Simon groaned when he saw the twins.

"I'll be the anchor," Robbie said, looping the rope around his waist. "You and these young ladies will do the tugging."

Simon shot Robbie a nasty look.

"It's just a suggestion," Robbie added. Simon nodded and got into position.

"Get ready," said the ref.

Simon smiled at the girls, then took hold of the rope.

"Everybody, dig your feet in!" Robbie

called as he leaned back on the rope. "Let's not give them an inch."

Then Robbie tried digging the treads of his sneakers into the grass, but he couldn't seem to get any traction.

Up in the bleachers, Lucy sized up the teams. As Robbie wrapped the rope around his waist, Lucy tapped Ruthie on the shoulder.

"My lips are a little chapped," she said. "Could you please lend me some lip balm?"

Ruthie blinked. "Er . . . I'm all out."

"What?" Lucy exclaimed. "How can that be? You must have had four or five jars of the stuff in that survival bag of yours."

Ruthie shrugged innocently. "I guess I used it all. This dry mountain air wreaks havoc on my delicate skin."

"What's the point of carrying a survival bag everywhere you go if you don't have the stuff you need when you need it?" Lucy demanded.

Ruthie smiled. "Believe me," she said. "I had what I needed, when I needed it."

"Quiet!" Mary shushed. "The tug-of-war is about to start."

As the ref prepared to give the signal, Lucy studied Ruthie, certain that her little sister was up to no good.

"GO!" the ref yelled.

Simon was jolted instantly as the other team yanked on the rope. He grunted and tugged, using all his weight. Robbie ground his heels into the dirt, but almost immediately his feet slipped in the grass, and he moved forward several inches.

"Dig in!" Simon called, his face red from exertion. The girls in front of Simon were tugging, too. But no matter how hard they pulled, inch by inch, Robbie, Simon, and the girls of Team Nine were being dragged toward the mud.

"This is too easy, right, Greta?"

"Right!" Greta laughed. "The competition is weak."

The Doublers' mocking words stung. "Put your back into it, Robbie!" Simon barked, redoubling his own efforts.

"It's not my back that's the problem," Robbie replied, still straining against the rope. "It's my feet. . . . I can't get any traction!"

There was another jolt, and Robbie

was dragged forward several more inches. He felt like he was on ice, the way his feet slipped along the grass.

The girls from Team Nine screamed just before their feet were dragged into the mud. They instantly let go of the rope and stepped away, before they could be plunged into the pit.

Without Team Nine, the game was over for Robbie and Simon, though they were too stubborn to give up. Within a few seconds, Simon tumbled headfirst into the mud. Robbie slipped to the ground, then was dragged into the pit, too. Both boys were plastered with mud.

"I can't see!" Simon cried.

"Wait a minute," Robbie said. He brushed huge chunks of wet, sticky muck away from Simon's face.

"That's better," Simon groaned, his blond hair dripping. "What happened?"

"Maybe you better bury your head in the mud again," Robbie warned. "Here come the Doubler twins."

"I didn't know American boys took mud baths," Erika jibed in a sing-song voice. "In my country, only girls do that! Your skin must be so soft and smooth. . . ."

Greta and Erika laughed. So did the guys who helped the Doubler twins to victory. Even the girls from Team Nine were giggling at their former partners' predicament.

The ref tapped the Doubler twins on the shoulders and pointed to the winner's circle.

"Over there! Collect your trophy," he said.

Then he looked down at Team Seven. "Since we're now on lunch break, you'll have time to clean up and get ready for the next event," the referee barked. "But if I were you, I'd give up."

Under his sticky coating of mud, Robbie blushed. Simon was still blinking mud out of his eyes. It was only then that Robbie noticed a sweet, fruity scent. It was coming from his shoes.

"What is that smell?" he asked.

Simon sniffed. "That's weird," he said. "It smells like cherries."

Robbie touched the bottom of his sneakers. Under the mud, they were covered with a slick, slimy gel.

"Whatever this smelly stuff is, it's all over the soles of my shoes. It's slippery, too.

No wonder I couldn't get any traction."

Simon rubbed some of the goo between his fingers, then sniffed it again. It smelled like wild cherries, all right—a scent that would appeal to a girl. He eyed the Doubler twins suspiciously as they stood in the winner's circle, accepting the winning trophy.

Could Greta and Erika be cheating? Simon wondered.

After they had showered and eaten, the boys contemplated their plans for the rest of the afternoon. "We missed the Frisbee toss, but the one-legged hop is up next," Robbie announced as he finished cleaning off his sneakers.

"What's the point?" Simon asked. "This isn't fun, and those girls are humiliating us—just like their cousins did."

"We can't back down now!" Robbie insisted. "We'll look like wimps."

"We look like jerks now," Simon shot back. "What's the difference? Maybe you should have partnered with Ruthie," Simon said with a sigh. "She really wanted to compete in the Big/Little Games, and I really didn't want to be here at all."

"There's always next year for Ruthie," Robbie replied. "This Oktoberfest, I have to help *you* out, whether you like it or not."

"And it's worked out great so far," Simon said bitterly.

"Come on, don't quit on me!"

Back at the playing field, the number of people in the bleachers had increased. The morning had turned to afternoon, and the sun was shining brightly. Many more competitors were lined up for the one-legged hop, too.

"Teams One through Fifteen, assemble at the starting line!" the ref cried after blowing his whistle. As Robbie and Simon moved into position, the ref gave them a sidelong glance that seemed to say *Don't you guys know when to quit?*

Robbie noticed the Doubler twins on the starting line, just a few feet away. The girls noticed he was watching, and giggled. Robbie felt a hot wave of anger and clenched his fist.

I'll show you.

"The rules are simple," the ref began. "When I say *go*, you start hopping toward the finish line on your right foot only. During the race, I will call for everyone to change to the left foot. Anyone who cannot keep up with my instructions will be disqualified.

"The first team member to cross the finish line takes the trophy for his partner, too."

Maybe I can win this one, even if Simon messes up again, Robbie thought.

"Tuck your left foot up and hold it with your left hand," the ref instructed.

When everyone was balanced on their right feet, he gave the signal.

"Ready . . . Set . . . GO!"

Everyone began to hop. Immediately, some contestants lost their balance and went tumbling. But Robbie and Simon moved quickly ahead, and within a few hops they were both in the lead.

"Go, Camden, go!" Robbie cried as he hopped along. He was out front, with Simon right behind him. The finish line got closer, but still seemed far away.

Then the ref's voice boomed through the bullhorn. "Switch to your left foot!"

Robbie dropped his left foot and raised his right, gripping it in his right hand. Then he began hopping again, still in the lead.

"Go, Robbie," Simon called. "I'm right behind you."

Suddenly a shaft of bright light stabbed into Robbie's eyes, blinding him. The intense glare was coming from a grove of pine trees just beyond the finish line.

"I . . . I can't see," Robbie huffed.

He tried to use his left hand to block out the light, but nearly lost his balance.

"Careful," Simon hissed. "You almost bumped into me."

Robbie lowered his left arm, and another brilliant beam of light struck his face. His eyes filled with tears and Robbie couldn't see the finish line. He began to drift to the right with every hop.

"Watch it!" Simon cried as Robbie crashed into him. They both fell down in a tangled heap. Lying on his back in the grass, Robbie watched the Doubler twins hop past them to be the first to cross the finish line.

The ref's whistle blew, signaling the end of competition.

"That's it!" Simon cried, his fist pounding the dirt. "I've had it."

"Sorry, but I was blinded—"

"I think it's more than that!" Simon

said, interrupting him. "I think you knew all along that those girls were the Doubler twins, and you got together with them to humiliate me in public!"

"What?" Robbie shouted. "That's crazy!"

"Is it?" Simon said, eyes flashing in anger. "I don't think so. You went out with those girls, you even said you *liked* them, yet you claim you didn't even know their last names."

"I didn't," Robbie protested.

"And I'm supposed to believe a guy who's dating the enemy?"

Simon jumped to his feet, dusted off his pants, and stalked away.

"I quit!" he called over his shoulder.

Robbie stumbled to his feet and brushed the grass off his clothes. He spotted the Doubler twins heading toward him, trophy in hand, and took off in the opposite direction. The last thing he needed right now were more jeers from those two!

And I thought girls were going to be easy to beat, Robbie remembered bitterly.

"Why is he running away?" Erika asked, disappointed. "I only wanted to see if he was hurt. He and Simon both took a bad fall."

Greta just shook her head. "I think they are cute—but weird, very weird."

"*Ja,*" Erika said, this time speaking German. "I don't think I will ever understand boys—especially American boys!"

In the middle of a thick grove of pine trees beyond the finish line, Ruthie was crouched behind some bushes. As she stood up, she thrust her makeup mirror back into her bag of tricks, smiling in triumph.

"Mission accomplished!" she crowed.

"That was a bad fall," Lucy said as she watched Simon and Robbie arguing.

Mary nodded. "They've had a lot of bad luck lately."

"I'm not sure luck had anything to do with it," Lucy said, thinking out loud.

"What do you mean?" said Mary. "Do you think it's fate or something?"

"Even worse," Lucy said. "Have you seen Ruthie lately?"

Mary shrugged. "Why?"

"I'm not sure—yet," Lucy replied. "But I have my suspicions."

"Fine," Mary said. "*You* can waste your whole trip figuring out what Ruthie is up to. I'm going to take a walk along the midway, where all the displays and games are set up."

SIX

After the one-legged hop, Simon wandered aimlessly, lost in thought. After a while, the anger he was feeling turned into shame and embarrassment.

How could I have been so stupid? he wondered.

In his heart of hearts, Simon knew that Robbie had nothing to do with their stinging defeats, and he also knew that Robbie would never try to humiliate him, or anyone—Robbie just wasn't like that.

So why did I even accuse him of it?

Simon realized it was probably because he was angry about losing to Doubler twins yet again.

And I thought girls would be easy to beat!

He wondered how he and Robbie ended up with a canvas sack with a hole in it, and how the slimy cherry stuff got on Robbie's sneakers, and if the Doublers had something to do with it. Though the Doubler twins weren't exactly the nicest girls in the world, Simon couldn't imagine that they would go so far as to cheat.

And to think, Simon reminded himself bitterly, *I actually kind of liked Greta when I first met her. Just goes to show you how wrong a first impression can be!*

The loud clang of a bell shook Simon out of his thoughts. He found himself walking along the Oktoberfest midway, where many game booths, displays, and volunteer recruitment stalls were set up. Hawkers called on people to try their luck at knocking down bowling pins with tennis balls, tossing a ring over a peg, or shooting plastic ducks with water guns—all to raise money for charity.

Once again, Simon heard the clang of the bell, and it jogged his memory. Aiming for the sound, Simon rounded a corner and spied a sign that read HAU DEN LUCAS—A TRADITIONAL OKTOBERFEST GAME IN BAVARIA.

Simon recognized the game at once.

Contestants hit a peg with a big wooden mallet, which in turn shot a metal "clanger" up a rail. If the contestant hit the peg hard enough, the clanger struck the bell at the top, and the winner got a prize.

The man running the booth spotted Simon. "Want to try your luck, kid?" he asked. "One try for a quarter."

Simon recalled the time that Matt tried to ring the bell. He lost—to Mary.

The man watched Simon, waiting for a reply. A person in the crowd cried, "I think he's chicken!"

I can't keep running from competition forever! Simon decided.

He fished into his pocket and handed the man a quarter. The man smiled and handed Simon the big wooden mallet.

Simon tested his grip, then raised the mallet high over his head. With all his might, he slammed it down on the peg. The clanger shot up the rail, stopping just short of the bell before gravity plunged it back down again.

"Nice try, kid," the man said sincerely. His kind words made Simon feel better about losing.

Maybe winning isn't everything, he decided. *Maybe just trying, doing my best, is good enough.*

Simon's thoughts were interrupted by a loud clang. Someone had hit the peg hard enough to ring the bell!

Simon turned to see Mary standing before him, one hand on her hip, the other spinning the mallet like it was a cheerleader's baton. She smiled and tossed the mallet to him. Simon caught it as Mary flexed her biceps.

"Maybe I should have become a fireman after all!" she gloated.

To Mary's surprise, Simon smiled. "Congratulations!" he said.

Mary's smug grin turned to a frown. "You're not mad?" she asked incredulously.

"Mad?" Simon replied. "Why should I be mad? It's just a game, and I did my best, which is more important than winning any day."

"That's . . . mature," Mary replied, a little disappointed that her brother would not take the bait.

"Have you seen Robbie?" Simon asked, checking his watch.

Mary shook her head.

"Well, if you do, tell him that I'll be waiting for my partner at the starting line. The treasure hunt begins in an hour, and I don't want to miss it!"

Standing unnoticed in the crowd, Ruthie rolled her eyes.

"Why can't you quit while you're ahead, Simon Camden?" she said.

Then the girl's eyes narrowed with determination. *I've been gentle so far,* she thought. *But now it's time for some drastic action.*

Still clutching her backpack, Ruthie hurried off to find Robbie before anyone else did.

"Here you are!" Ruthie said as she entered Simon and Robbie's tent. "I've been looking all over for you."

"Hey, Ruthie," Robbie replied. He was stretched out on his cot, a frown plastered on his face.

"Tough day?" Ruthie asked.

Robbie sat up. "You could say that."

"Well," Ruthie continued. "I could have

told you this would happen. But not to worry—there's still hope. The Big/Little Games are still going on—if we leave now, we can just make the jump-rope competition!"

"Thanks, but no thanks," Robbie said.

Ruthie frowned.

"I'm really sorry about missing the Big/Little Games," Robbie continued. "I know you were disappointed, and you've been a really good sport about the situation. Next year, it's you and me. We'll enter all the competitions and we'll win, too. I promise."

Ruthie continued to frown. "What about this year?"

Robbie held Ruthie's shoulders and looked her in the eyes. "You know that I have to be a big brother for Simon . . . even if he doesn't want me to. So I'm going to wait right here until he gets back, and talk him into competing one last time."

"Are you sure?" Ruthie asked.

Robbie nodded.

"Absolutely, positively, cross-your-heart sure?"

"Yeah, Ruthie, I'm sure," Robbie said. "That's the way it's got to be."

"Okay," Ruthie said with a sigh. "If it's got to be that way, then it's got to be that way."

Ruthie fumbled in her bag until her hand closed on the right object. Smiling, she handed Robbie a compass in a protective leather pouch.

"What's this?"

"My lucky Brownie compass," Ruthie explained. "Simon said he would be waiting for you at the treasure hunt's starting line. And if you're going on a treasure hunt, then you're going to need a compass, right?"

Robbie jumped to his feet. "Simon really said that?"

Ruthie nodded.

"Then I'd better get over there! The hunt starts any minute now. . . ."

He looked down at Ruthie. "Thanks for the compass," he said. "It really means a lot to me. I'll never forget how generous you were today."

Ruthie suddenly had second thoughts.

"Wait!" she cried. "I have to tell you something before you go."

"No time," Robbie said as he raced out of the tent.

Alone in the tent, Ruthie threw up her arms and sighed.

"I tried to warn him. . . ."

Ruthie left the boys' tent and crossed the festival grounds to the girls' campground. She entered her own tent, kicked off her shoes, and dumped her pink bag in the corner.

"Now that my plan is working, I'm not so sure I want it to," she said out loud.

"What plan is that?"

Ruthie turned and saw Lucy standing inside the tent.

"I . . . I thought I was alone," Ruthie stammered.

"I'll bet you did," Lucy replied with a hint of aggravation. She was clutching a book in her hands, and Ruthie could read the big red letters on the cover, even from across the tent: *The Kids' Guide to Really Cool Practical Jokes.*

"This book makes for some interesting reading," Lucy said, staring at her little sister. "I especially like the part about the slippery stuff on the shoes."

Ruthie slumped onto her cot and covered her face with the pillow.

"Busted!" she moaned.

. . .

"The treasure hunt lasts for approximately two hours," the referee explained, his voice booming through the bullhorn. "In that time you are to follow the map until you locate something that looks like this. . . ."

The referee held up a bright orange soccer ball with a smiley face painted on it, eliciting laughs from the crowd.

"Each of the twelve teams will be given a compass and a map. Teams One through Four will travel along the East Trail. Teams Five through Eight will take the North Trail. The rest of you will go South.

"There is one of these"—he held up the ball again—"hidden somewhere along each of the three trails. The first team to locate an orange ball and bring it back to camp will be declared the winner."

Another referee walked along the line, distributing photocopied maps. When he got to Team Seven, he handed Robbie a copy. He offered them a compass, too, but Robbie held up the one Ruthie loaned him.

"Thanks, but I have my own," he said.

"This shouldn't be too hard," the referee told the boys. "Just walk due north, follow the trail, your compass, and the map. There are several forks in the path. Each time you reach a fork, just go north and you'll do fine. Good luck."

"Thanks," said Simon.

The ref moved along to the next team and gave them the same talk.

Simon noticed that Robbie seemed a little tense. "You're not still upset about the things I said, are you?" Simon asked. "I already apologized."

"No way!" Robbie replied. "Apology accepted. I just don't like the woods very much. I guess I'm a city boy at heart."

Simon chuckled. "Don't worry, this is a national park." There are people everywhere, park rangers, and the trails are pretty easy to follow. And don't forget," Simon added. "We have a map and a compass, too."

Robbie shrugged. "I guess you're right."

"Hey, Robbie! Simon!"

The boys turned and saw the Doubler twins waving to them. The girls were wearing hiking boots, and had their map and compass.

"Don't get lost now," Erika said, wagging her finger at them.

"And don't let any nasty old bears eat you, either," said Greta.

"You know what," Robbie muttered under his breath. "I don't think I like those girls very much."

One referee stood at the start of each trail. "Teams One through Four, up to the line!" one of them shouted.

"Teams Five through Eight, over here," called another. Robbie and Simon jogged up to the base of the North Trail. The Doubler twins—Team Six—were there, too. Simon and Robbie tried to ignore the girls and concentrate on the contest at hand.

When all three groups were poised at the base of their trails, a referee with a stopwatch raised his hand.

"Ready . . . Set . . . Go!"

As fast as they could run, Robbie and Simon took off down the trail. They ran and ran, hopping over fallen logs, ducking under low-hanging branches, following the twisting trail until they left everyone else in the dust. They didn't even slow down when they hit forks in the trail. Robbie just checked his compass on the fly and pointed north as they kept on going.

"We can slow down now," Simon said between breaths. "I think we finally lost them."

Robbie slowed to a quick walk as he scanned the forest around him.

The late-afternoon sun started to wane, and the air became a little bit colder. Soon the wind increased. Robbie shivered and zipped his jacket up to his neck. After twenty minutes, they hit a new fork on the path.

"Check the compass," Simon suggested. Robbie looked at the dial.

"If we go this way, we're good," he declared, turning down a path. "We're heading due north, just like the ref told us to."

"Let's walk a little faster," Simon suggested. "We don't want anyone—especially the Doubler twins—to catch up to us."

Together, Robbie and Simon hurried forward, their feet crushing through the bushes as they darted down the new trail. All the time, the boys kept following the compass.

Mary was singing happily to herself when she got back to her tent. A frowning Ruthie and an annoyed Lucy greeted her.

"We've got a problem," Lucy announced, handing Mary the practical joke book. "Check out page 27, the fishhook stunt. And page 99, the grease on the shoes—"

"It was lip balm," Ruthie protested.

"Whatever!" Lucy replied before turning to Mary. "Can you believe that Ruthie has been pulling these stunts all day?"

Mary laughed. "You've got to admit. It *is* pretty funny!"

A look of pride crossed Ruthie's face.

"But," Mary added sternly, "Simon and Robbie are going to be really mad when they find out about this."

"*If* they find out," said Lucy. "They have to get back from the treasure hunt in the woods first."

"What do you mean?" Mary asked.

Lucy shot another look at Ruthie, who

suddenly seemed very interested in her shoes.

"Oh, it gets worse," Lucy explained. "Check out the 'practical joke' on page 118."

Mary flipped to the page, scanned it, then looked up at Lucy.

"Oh, no," Mary groaned. Then she looked at Ruthie. "You *did* this?"

Ruthie nodded.

"We have to do something!" Mary cried out in alarm.

"I agree," said Lucy.

"What's the big deal?" Ruthie asked with a shrug.

"The big deal is that we're in the mountains," Lucy explained. "People get lost in the forest all the time. Sometimes people even get hurt!"

"But it was just a prank," Ruthie insisted, her brow furrowed. "A practical joke."

"A joke that could hurt someone," Mary insisted. "Maybe even get someone killed."

"Let's go find the counselors," Lucy said. "They'll know what to do."

"I'm coming, too," Ruthie declared, suddenly worried.

"Oh, no, you are most definitely *not*," Lucy told her. "You will sit down and wait here until Mary and I, as your official surrogate parents for the weekend, figure out a way to punish you for this stupid, dangerous prank!"

SEVEN

The sun had nearly set. The mountains in the distance began to fade in the darkness, until only their frosting of white snow was visible. Robbie and Simon pushed their way through a thick tangle of bushes, searching desperately for an easier path through the woods.

"There has to be an easier trail around here somewhere," Simon said. "The ref told us there was."

Robbie eyed the thick foliage and tall trees all around them.

"I don't think this is the trail we were supposed to follow. In fact, I don't see any trail at all," he said ominously. "But we've been going north at each fork—just like they told us to."

Simon scanned the area. Robbie was right. There was no path, no trail, no sign of civilization at all.

"We've been walking for almost two hours," he said. "We should have found the soccer ball, or seen another team, or something! We must have gotten off the trail somehow. Gone in the wrong direction . . ."

Robbie sighed. "Not according to the compass. We've been walking due north the whole time."

"Well," Simon said, wiping the sweat from his forehead. "We are definitely lost. Maybe that compass is broken. Maybe it was sabotaged by the Doubler twins."

"Don't start that again!" Robbie exclaimed. "Those two girls never got near this compass. It belongs to Ruthie and—"

Robbie's mouth snapped shut, and he slapped his forehead. "How could I have been so stupid?" he moaned.

"What?"

Robbie didn't reply. Instead, he began fumbling with the compass, trying to remove it from its protective leather pouch.

"What's going on?" Simon demanded. But Robbie continued to fumble with their only compass.

"Think about it," Robbie said. "A hole in our canvas sack . . . cherry goo on my shoes. Goo that smells suspiciously like—"

Simon snapped his fingers. "Like Ruthie's wild cherry lip balm!"

"Exactly," Robbie said. "And then Ruthie gives me this . . . her 'good-luck' compass! I'm sure this compass must be—"

Robbie finally ripped the compass out of its pouch. Inside the protective holder, he spied a pink plastic bunny with a magnet for a back.

"—sabotaged with a refrigerator magnet."

As Robbie pulled off the magnet, the compass needle, now free of the magnet's pull, swung on its axis until it pointed due north. North, as it turned out, was at a 90° angle to the direction they had been walking—the boys had been going in the wrong direction for two whole hours!

Simon and Robbie exchanged terrified glances.

"We *are* lost!" they cried out in unison.

From somewhere in the deep forest that surrounded them, a coyote howled at the setting sun.

The state trooper snapped his notebook closed and gazed at Mary, Lucy, Reverend Gerst, and the camp counselors.

"What about the other teams?" the trooper asked.

"They're all back, safe and sound," Reverend Gerst replied. "All but Team Seven—Robbie Palmer and Simon Camden."

The trooper tilted his hat back and scratched his forehead. "It will be dark soon, so I'm going to issue an APB—"

"A what?" Lucy said nervously.

"An all-points bulletin," the trooper explained. "This bulletin will describe the boys and warn all state and local police and park rangers to be on the lookout for two lost teenagers. If we still haven't found them by morning, we'll send out the dogs."

"Oh, no," Ruthie whimpered.

"Don't worry," the state trooper added. "Usually lost kids turn up in a few hours. If they aren't found in that period of time, then . . ."

The officer paused, wary of alarming the girls even more.

"Well, let's just hope we find those boys," he concluded.

"It's going to get really dark soon," Robbie said.

"And cold!" Simon added. "Really, really cold."

Robbie paled. "I don't want to die out here! I have plenty to live for."

"You're not going to die," said Simon. "I'm sure Reverend Gerst has already called for help. There's probably a search party looking for us right now."

"But where are they going to search?" Robbie demanded. "They think we went north, but we really went west—or at least I think it was west."

"Don't panic," said Simon. "That's the most important thing. We have to keep cool heads."

Whoooooooooo!

"What's that!" Robbie cried out in alarm.

"An owl. I'm sure it's an owl," Simon said tensely.

Suddenly the bushes near the boys began to rustle. They both crouched down behind a fallen log.

"What's that!" Robbie hissed, his voice a frightened whisper.

"I don't know," Simon hissed back. "Maybe a bird? Maybe a fox?"

"Or maybe a bear!" Robbie moaned.

The rustling got louder. Simon and Robbie watched the bushes move. There was something behind those bushes—something wild and alive and coming toward them. From behind the leaves, the boys heard animal sounds.

Robbie cracked first.

"It's a bear! Run!" he cried as he leaped to his feet. He crashed through the foliage, vanishing from sight.

"Wait for me," Simon yelled as he followed Robbie. The animal behind them began moving, too. It was still following the boys.

Robbie burst through a final tangle of bushes and stumbled as the ground fell away under his feet. He rolled down an embankment just as Simon crashed through the trees above him. With a surprised cry,

Simon fell over the embankment, too. They both landed on their backs—hard.

To their surprise, Simon and Robbie found themselves stretched out on a paved road. In the distance they could see an all-night convenience store, with pickup trucks and recreational vehicles parked around it.

Then the boys saw a raccoon staring down at them from the top of the embankment, its nose twitching in curiosity.

Just then, a police car rounded the corner and rolled to a halt. Simon and Robbie rose to their feet as the driver rolled down his window.

"Are you Simon Camden and Robbie Palmer?" the state trooper asked.

Robbie and Simon nodded in relief.

"Hop in," the officer commanded. "There are some people worried about you."

The drive back to the Oktoberfest site took less than twenty minutes. As the state police car rolled through the gate, Robbie and Simon spotted the Doubler twins. Erika triumphantly held an orange soccer ball over her head.

"They won again," Simon noted.

"Great!" Robbie replied. "I'm happy for

them. But I'm even happier to be out of the woods!"

"I'm so glad you're all right!" Lucy cried when they were reunited. She and Mary hugged them both.

"Ruthie confessed to everything," Lucy explained. "She ripped your sack with a fishhook, put the lip balm on Robbie's shoes, reflected the sun off her makeup mirror to blind Robbie during the one-legged race, and placed the refrigerator magnet inside the compass case so you'd go in the wrong direction!"

"I feel terrible," Robbie said, shaking his head. "Like I drove Ruthie to do these things because I disappointed her."

"It's not your fault," Mary insisted. "Ruthie always resorts to pranks to get attention."

"I'll say," Lucy added. "Remember when she told her teacher that Mom and Dad were getting a divorce!"

"So what do we do about it?" Robbie asked.

Mary's eyes twinkled. "Don't worry," she chuckled. "Lucy and I have devised a suitable punishment."

Simon and Robbie followed Mary and Lucy to the center of the midway. A sign over a crowded booth read DUNK THIS PRANKSTER FOR CHARITY—JUST 25 CENTS. Inside, sitting on a hard wooden bench, was Ruthie, her feet dangling over a plastic swimming pool filled with water.

Mary dropped a quarter into the pot and handed Robbie a baseball. "Hit the target, and down she goes," Mary said.

Robbie stepped up to the booth, gripping the ball. When Ruthie spied him, her eyes went wide.

"Wait!" she cried. "Let's make a deal. If you drop that ball and walk away, we'll call it even—you don't even have to partner with me at next year's Oktoberfest."

Robbie made a big show of thinking about it. "No," he said at last. "I'll partner with you—just like I promised."

Then Robbie took careful aim, and threw the baseball as hard as he could. He hit the bull's-eye, dead on, and the seat dropped out from under Ruthie. With a squeal and a splash, she plunged into the chilly water.

"It feels good to win at last," Robbie said with a big smile.

EIGHT

When they returned to their tent, Simon and Robbie found two tickets for the hayride on their cots, with a note from Ruthie.

"Dear Simon and Robbie," Ruthie's note began. "I am sorry that you got lost in the woods. I am sorry you lost all the games. I was the one who set everything up so you would fail. I want you both to know that you could have easily beaten those Doubler twins—Evan and Gerhart, or Greta and Erika—except that I messed you both up. To prove that I am sorry, I used my allowance to buy you tickets to the hayride. Have fun."

"Signed, Ruthie," Robbie read with a

sigh. "I guess she feels pretty bad."

Simon grinned. "Pretty *wet*, too!"

"Well, it was nice of her to get us tickets to the hayride," Robbie said. "I thought it was sold out."

"At least something is going right today," Simon said. "And I know we'll have fun tonight."

The boys changed their clothes and headed off to the hayride, arriving just seconds before the last wagon pulled out. The Doubler twins were waiting for them.

"We've been hoping you would show up, but we weren't sure the police would find you in time!" Erika exclaimed.

"Hello, Simon," Greta said, smiling warmly.

Erika offered Robbie her hand. He took it and climbed onto the wagon. Robbie and Erika sat down together in the hay, Simon and Greta nearby.

"I guess congratulations are in order," Robbie said. "You girls won every event."

Erika flexed her muscles. "We Doublers are very competitive. I warned you."

Simon laughed for the first time that weekend. "Are there any more Doubler twins out there?"

Greta nodded. "Our little cousins, Inga and Olga, live in Glenoak. But they are only two years old."

"I'll warn Sam and David," said Simon. Robbie chuckled.

"So why are you being so nice?" Robbie asked. "I thought you didn't like us."

"That's not true," Erika replied. "My sister and I think you are very cute."

"Then why did you give us such a hard time on the playing field?"

Erika laughed. "We had to get your attention, didn't we?"

Erika and Robbie were soon lost in conversation. As the wagon rumbled down the trail, Greta curled her arm around Simon's.

"Robbie told me all about you," she said. "He says you are very smart, and that he likes you very much. . . ."

"I like him, too," Simon replied. "Robbie is like a big brother to me. He's not perfect, but he tries really hard because he cares, and that's what's important."

Lucy and Mary watched as the wagon disappeared down the trail.

"I can't believe you sold Ruthie our hayride tickets," said Lucy.

"I can't believe Ruthie was so apologetic that she bought them!" Mary replied.

Lucy stared down the trail. "After all that they've been through, the boys deserve a good time."

"Robbie and Simon will have more fun than we would have. After all, how much fun is a hayride without a date?" said Mary. Then she tapped her pocket. "And with Ruthie's allowance, we can find our own fun tonight."

"It's amazing," Lucy said. "Those girls beat Simon and Robbie at every event—and even made fun of them. Now they are acting like Simon and Robbie are the men of their dreams."

"It *does* make you think," Mary said.

"Think what?"

"That if two losers like Robbie and Simon can find dates—then there must be hope for everybody."

Lucy grabbed Mary's arm. "You're absolutely right!" she said with a nod. "Let's go!"

SISTERS THROUGH
THE SEASONS

ONE

"Wow! Would you look at that?"

Lucy Camden leaned across her sister Mary, and looked out the window of their cab. The cab was crossing a bridge into New York City. Across the water towered the skyscrapers of midtown Manhattan. It was late November, and the afternoon light glittered off thousands of windows.

"I mean, I'm not easily impressed, but that's incredible," Mary said. "Don't you think?"

"Yeah," Lucy agreed. "Beautiful."

"I feel like I could look at that forever," Mary said.

Lucy was silent; she had seen the view before. That time she'd been in a cab going the opposite direction. She'd been *fleeing* the city and leaving behind her engagement to Jeremy and her future at seminary school.

Lucy sighed and sat back. The memories hurt. Her brief stint in the city hadn't been a good time for her. But this visit to New York would be different. She and Mary were on their way to Buffalo, to spend Thanksgiving with the Colonel. They'd flown into New York City because Mary had gotten a cheap fare. The girls figured they could do some Christmas shopping in the city and catch a train to Buffalo the next day.

Lucy was looking forward to hanging out in New York. This trip was an opportunity for her and Mary to spend some time together. Although neither of them had admitted it, things hadn't been very good between them ever since Mary had come back home from Buffalo.

Mary had been looking forward to the trip for just the same reason. She was also excited about tonight. Mary loved her sister very much, and, even though she didn't like to admit it, actually looked up to her in a lot of ways. But Mary felt that if there was one thing she could teach Lucy, it was how to loosen up and have a good time. What could be better for that than a night in New York City?

Mary grinned and turned to Lucy. But Lucy was staring listlessly out the window.

"Hey," Mary said. "What's wrong?"

Lucy shook her head. "Nothing," she said. "Just old memories."

Then Mary remembered. *Duh!* she thought. "Is it Jeremy?" she asked.

Lucy gave a wan smile and nodded.

Mary slung her arm over her sister's shoulders. "Forget it," she said. "You and I are going to have a *great* time on this trip. Who cares about stupid old Jeremy?"

"I know," Lucy said. "I'll be okay."

Mary nodded. "You just wait," she said. "I've got a feeling tonight is going to be one to remember."

Lucy nodded as Mary turned back to the window. *I hope so,* she thought. But inside she felt a twinge of nervousness. Despite all her time in Buffalo learning to be responsible, Mary didn't seem all that different. And now Lucy was trusting her to take care of all tonight's arrangements.

It's not like I had a lot of choice, Lucy thought. The only people she knew in the city were Jeremy and his folks, and there was no way she was getting in touch with them, let alone asking them if she and Mary could spend the night. So instead they were staying with a friend of Mary's, a girl she had known in Buffalo.

"Where does this girl live again?" Lucy asked, glancing back out the window. They were across the bridge and had turned south on one of the city's avenues. Other cars jockeyed for position all around them, horns blowing.

"Her name's Delia," Mary said. "And she's totally cool. I think you're actually going to like her. She's going to art school and is living someplace called the East Village."

The East Village, Lucy thought with a shudder. *Right.* She knew about the East Village. The three months she was in the city, she'd pointedly never visited the neighborhood. It had always sounded just a bit too wild for her taste. *Just like Jeremy,* she found herself thinking.

Outside, the lights of the city were starting to blink on. Streetlights, shop windows, and, higher up, apartment windows. Many of the windows were decorated with bright holiday lights.

For a while, they were stopped dead in traffic. On the other side of the clear plastic divider between the driver and the backseat, their cabbie was shaking his head and mumbling to himself.

"What's the problem?" Mary asked amiably.

The cabbie glanced back at them. "Rush-hour traffic," he explained.

"Oh," Mary said.

Suddenly the driver saw an opening. He spun the wheel and accelerated, and Mary was thrown back in her seat.

The driver swore and pounded the steering wheel when another driver beat him to the opening.

Lucy clutched at Mary's arm. "Maybe coming into the city wasn't such a great idea," she said.

"What, are you kidding?" Mary said. "This is great! This is the real thing! You don't get any more New York City than this."

Yeah, right, Lucy thought. *If Mary was loving it so much, why'd she look so pale?*

After another agonizing half hour creeping through traffic, they finally broke free of it and sailed down the avenue.

"What's the address?" the driver called back.

"Hold on a minute," Mary said, digging through her backpack. She found a scrap of paper and read from it. "167 East 7th Street."

The driver nodded. Lucy leaned back and watched the avenue roll by. It wasn't long before she started to think maybe they had entered the East Village. At the next stoplight, a group of greasy-looking guys with guitars on their backs crossed in front of them. Right behind them were a couple of girls her age with fluorescent green hair, torn fishnet stockings, and nose rings. Walking behind them was a perfectly normal-looking old lady, stooped over and walking with a cane.

"Weird," Lucy said.

"Pretty cool people, huh?" Mary said.

"I don't know," Lucy said. "I feel a little nervous about staying here. Are you sure it's okay?"

Mary looked at her sister in surprise. "Are you kidding?"

Lucy just raised her eyebrows.

"Hey, this is going to be a *lot* of fun. Trust me!"

I'm trying, Lucy thought.

Five minutes later, their cab turned onto a side street and pulled to the curb.

"Here we are!" Mary said, craning across the seat to see Delia's building. "Come on, let's go."

"Don't we need to pay the driver?" Lucy suggested quietly.

"Oh, right!" Mary said. "Duh. I'll take care of it."

She started scrounging around in her backpack for her purse. After a moment, she paused and looked guiltily at Lucy. "Um . . . I only have two dollars." She held up two crumpled dollar bills.

Lucy sighed. "Am I supposed to be surprised?" she asked. Lucy dug her wallet out of her backpack and paid the driver, then they retrieved their duffel bags from the trunk.

"So," Mary said. "Here we are!"

They looked around. The street was lined with trees, the leaves of which had turned bright autumn golds and reds. The gutter was littered with those that had already fallen. Behind the trees were old-looking buildings, all about five or six stories tall. Many of them had a shop on the ground floor, with a brightly lit window and awning. Lucy saw a couple of funky-looking clothes shops, a bookstore, and a small restaurant or two. Small groups of people strolled down the sidewalks, talking and laughing in the cold. Everyone was wearing winter coats, and their breath was clouding the air.

Lucy shivered. It was much colder than she'd expected!

"Come on," Mary said. "Let's go up to Delia's apartment."

They turned and walked up a set of steps to the building's front door. Mary pulled on the door, but it was locked.

Huh? she thought. *How were people supposed to get in?*

"Here," Lucy said, scanning a list of names next to the door. "In New York the building doors are always locked. Unless you have a doorman, of course. What apartment is Delia in?"

Mary dug through her backpack again for the sheet of paper with Delia's address. "Uh . . . 7A," she finally said.

"7A . . . ," Lucy said, running her finger down the list. "Here it is." Lucy pressed a button, and a buzzing sound came out of a speaker next to the list.

"That's ringing up in Delia's apartment," Lucy explained. "She can press a button up there and talk to us through this intercom, and then open the door."

Mary raised her eyebrows in surprise. Who knew security in New York was so tight? Even more, who would expect Lucy Camden to know her way around things like that? *Well, she* did *live here for three months,* Mary reminded herself.

She gave Lucy a sly grin and playfully punched her on the arm. "You're such a sophisticated New Yorker!"

Lucy tossed her hair over her shoulder and batted her eyelashes. "Darling!" she said breathlessly.

The sisters laughed. They looked at the speaker expectantly.

After a few moments Lucy asked, "She knows we're coming, right?"

"Yeah," Mary said. "I talked to her last week about it. It's all set. I told you, I took care of everything."

Lucy buzzed 7A again, trying to ignore

the sinking sensation in her stomach. She was suddenly feeling incredibly exposed, standing in front of a locked door on a New York City street. Did they look vulnerable? Were they incredibly obvious? If Delia wasn't home, what were they supposed to do?

Beside her, Mary was fidgeting. This didn't look good. She *had* talked to Delia, just like she'd said, but it wasn't like any of her friends were particularly responsible.

Mary glanced at her sister worriedly. If Delia had forgotten and wasn't home, it wasn't going to be a good start for her and Lucy's trip together.

Lucy was about to buzz again when a crackling came from the speaker and a sleepy voice asked, "Hello?"

Lucy and Mary each felt a wave of relief.

"Uh . . . hello?" Mary said, leaning forward awkwardly. "Delia? It's Mary and Lucy Camden."

"Who?" the voice asked.

TWO

"It's Mary. Mary Camden?" Mary said again.

There was no reply, but after a moment, there was a buzzing sound and they heard the door click. Lucy shoved it open before it could lock again.

They stepped into the building. On the other side of a small entryway was another door. Lucy darted forward and opened that a moment before the buzzing stopped.

Lucy found herself in a grungy, dimly lit hallway.

Mary grinned. *It's so Bohemian!* she thought excitedly.

At the end of the hall was a red door with a circular window in it.

"Is that the elevator?" Lucy asked.

"I think so," Mary said. "Look. Here's the call button."

Mary pressed a button next to the door, and they heard a motor somewhere nearby start up. While it droned away, Lucy noticed full garbage bags piled in the corner next to the elevator. *Ugh!* she thought. Images of cockroaches jumped to mind. She turned away from the bags and focused on the elevator door. While she watched, the car moved down past the round window, lighting it up. Then the engine sound cut out, and they heard a brief rattling.

The sisters looked at each other. "Why do I feel like this elevator is even more dangerous than the cab from the airport?" Lucy asked.

"We could take the stairs," Mary suggested.

Lucy checked out the stairs. They looked steep and dark. She shook her head and motioned to the elevator. "I'm game if you are."

Mary pulled open the door and revealed the smallest elevator car Lucy had ever seen. It looked like a closet! They stepped inside and let the door swing shut behind them. To the right of the door was a panel with buttons. Lucy pressed 7. As soon as she did, a metal gate automatically folded across the door—that had been the rattling sound they'd heard. With a clunk and a drone, the elevator started up. It really was like being in a moving closet, Lucy thought. Only the metal gate stood between them and the building's wall. They watched door after door slowly pass by, each marked with the floor's number.

Mary glanced at her sister and wisely kept her mouth shut. But to her the elevator seemed so interesting! No elevator she'd ever been in had been even remotely like this!

Finally, they arrived at 7, and the metal gate drew back with a screech.

"Here we are!" Mary said brightly. She pushed open the door, and they exited into a hall much like the one downstairs.

"7A . . . ," Mary said aloud. There was no indication whatsoever which direction that might be. The hall branched in two directions; at the end of each of those branches were two more. They wandered down one hall, and then another. Behind the doors they heard dogs barking, TVs blaring, and people talking.

Finally, they doubled back and stopped in front of a door they'd passed before and disregarded. It didn't have a number, but it was the only one left. Lucy looked closely and saw 7A scratched into the paint.

"I guess this is it," she said. She knocked on the door. The knock echoed in the hall, sounding jarringly loud.

On the other side of the door they heard the sound of someone moving around.

"Who is it?" the person asked.

The sisters looked at each other. "Delia?" Mary called.

Lucy was painfully aware of their loud voices. She had the uneasy feeling that people behind the other doors were listening to them.

"Delia, it's me, Mary Camden," Mary said warmly, "and my sister Lucy. Remember? I talked to you last week?"

There was the sound of locks being turned, and the door opened an inch. The room behind the door was dark. A cute girl with disheveled blond hair peered out at them.

"Mary?" the girl said.

Lucy felt both relieved and irritated. *Finally!* she thought.

"Delia, hey," Mary said, giving her a grin. "Do you think we could come in?"

"Oh, I'm sorry," Delia said. She closed the door for a moment and undid the chain, then opened the door wide. "Come on in!"

Lucy and Mary stepped past the girl into the dim apartment. Behind them Delia closed the door and started locking up again.

"So what are you guys doing here?"

Lucy froze. She was glad it was dark, because the look on her face was frosty.

Oh, great, Mary thought, looking warily at her sister. "Uh . . . we're here for the evening, on our way to Buffalo. Remember? I talked to you last week, and you said we could stay with you . . . ?"

"Oh, right!" Delia said. She turned on a light. "I remember now. I thought that was next week, right before Thanksgiving."

"Thanksgiving is this week," Mary reminded her.

"Oh, is it Thanksgiving already?" Delia asked. She laughed. "I just can't keep track. No, I thought you were coming for that visit next week."

"You see," Lucy interrupted, "we're on our way to Buffalo to spend the holiday with a relative. So *that's* why we're here now."

"Oh . . . ," Delia said. "I get it."

Mary frowned at Lucy. *Don't be rude!* she thought. Then she introduced her to Delia.

Delia smiled at Lucy. "I'm sorry the place is such a mess. If I'd known you were coming, I'd have cleaned up a bit!"

Lucy restrained herself from pointing out that she *should have* known they were coming.

"I think it's great," Mary said. To Mary the disorder seemed casual and inviting.

Delia darted around the apartment, pushing clothes off the futon and chairs.

She's cute, Lucy admitted to herself, *in a perky sort of way.* Delia was about the same height as Lucy and was wearing sweatpants and a T-shirt.

"Make yourselves at home," she said. "Just drop your bags anywhere."

"Thanks," Mary said, putting her bag down and collapsing onto the futon. "Cool place!"

"Thanks," Delia said, disappearing down a hall to the left.

Cool place? Lucy thought incredulously. It was a mess. Not even Simon's and Matt's rooms, on their worst days, could rival it. Other than the futon, the only furniture were two chairs and an old ottoman, which seemed to serve as a coffee table. There was a small TV against the opposite wall. To the right was a window looking out over the street, and to the left was the hall down which Delia had just disappeared.

At least it's warm, Lucy thought. Out loud she said, "What a dump!"

Mary looked shocked. "What are you talking about?" she said. "This is great! You don't get more New York than this!"

"Great?" Lucy asked. "I'm afraid to touch anything in here, it's that dirty!"

"Be nice," Mary said. "I mean, she *is* letting us stay with her."

Lucy glared at her sister. "This is a *disaster!*" she hissed. "I don't want to spend another *minute* in this place!"

From the other end of the apartment, Delia called, "What can I get you girls to drink? I've got water, water, and . . . water!"

Hilarious, Lucy thought.

Mary laughed. "Perfect!"

"Coming right up!" Delia called. "Now, let's see . . . all I need are a couple of clean glasses. . . ."

Lucy rolled her eyes.

"Look, where do you want to go? Do you want to call Jeremy?" Mary asked. Sometimes Lucy could be so ungracious!

"Of course not," Lucy said.

"And it's not like we've got the money for a hotel."

Lucy sighed. Mary had her there. Scrunching her eyes shut, Lucy put down her bag, turned, and sat down next to Mary on the futon.

"See? That wasn't so bad, was it?" Mary asked, enjoying her sister's discomfort.

"I don't know," Lucy said, "I haven't inhaled yet."

"Here we are!" Delia said, coming back into the room. "Two waters!"

Delia handed Mary a tall glass with an image of Mickey Mouse on one side and Donald Duck on the other.

"Thanks," Mary said.

To Lucy, Delia held out a green ceramic coffee mug.

Lucy eyed it dubiously. "Uh . . . thanks, but I'm fine," she said.

"Oh," Delia said. "Okay. Well, let me know if you change your mind." She turned and went back to the kitchen.

Mary whacked Lucy on the leg. "What are you doing!" she hissed.

"There was *no way* I was touching that mug, let alone drink anything out of it. Do you think she cleaned it? *I* didn't hear the faucet."

"I can't believe you," Mary said. "You're so spoiled!"

"And you're so irresponsible!" Lucy shot back. "I can't believe I trusted you to set this up."

Mary glared at her sister. She was about to say something back when Delia came into the room. She slid into one of the two battered chairs.

"Whew! I'm beat. I was out a little late last night," she confided.

"Sounds fun," Mary said, suddenly worried that Delia would be too tired to go out tonight. *What am I worried about?*

Mary thought. *This is Delia we're talking about here! She could party every night for a week straight!*

Delia grinned. "It was." Then her grin faltered. "At least, what I can remember of it."

Delia shook her head, as if to clear it, then gave Mary a big smile. "It's so good to see you! How are you?"

Lucy just sat while Mary and Delia caught up. Lucy eyed the walls—Delia had paintings hanging up.

Lucy got up and walked over to take a look. There were four paintings in the corner. All of them seemed to be close-ups of individual flowers with vibrant, rich colors.

"Who painted these?" Lucy asked.

Delia turned from her conversation with Mary. She smiled. "I did. What do you think?"

Lucy's eyes widened in surprise. She looked back at the paintings. "I love them," she admitted. And she did. "They're beautiful."

Delia grinned shyly. "Thanks. Hey, are you guys hungry? Do you want to get some food?"

"Are you kidding?" Mary said. "All I've

had today is airplane food! Let's eat!"

For a horrible moment, Lucy thought Delia was suggesting cooking something in the kitchen. *If the living room is this messy,* Lucy thought, *I don't even want to see the kitchen!*

"Um . . . ," she said.

"There's a great Thai place right down the street," Delia offered.

Thank goodness, Lucy thought. "Sounds great!" she said brightly.

Over Delia's shoulder, Mary frowned at her sister. She knew what she had been thinking. Out loud Mary said, "Let's do it!"

"Great!" said Delia, bouncing out of her seat. "Let me just brush my hair and change my clothes. . . ." She disappeared down the hall.

Mary gave her sister a death glare. "If you don't start being nice to Delia," she said, "I'm going to make you regret it."

THREE

The restaurant *was* just down the street. That was one of the very cool things about New York, Mary thought. Delia had told her all about it—a half a block from your house you could find almost everything you might need—laundry, restaurants, shops.

The restaurant was small; Mary thought there might be ten tables in the whole place. On the walls hung red- and yellow-colored silks; bamboo plants grew from pots along the wall.

Mary felt a thrill of excitement run through her. The place was so different than any restaurant she'd ever been in before!

They sat down at a table halfway back. Right away a waitress came over with menus and asked if they wanted anything to drink.

"Oooh," Delia said. She closed her eyes. "Tonight I think I'll start with . . . a Coconut Sling." She opened her eyes and grinned at them. "It's delicious!"

"Mmmm . . . ," Mary said, intending to order the same thing. "I'll have—"

"Water!" Lucy interjected. "She'll have water, and so will I."

The waitress nodded and walked off. Mary glared at Lucy. *Couldn't she just relax?* Mary wondered.

"Water?" Delia asked. "Are you guys on a diet or something?"

"Something like that," Lucy said. *If you consider not drinking alcohol a diet,* she thought. "Coconut Sling" sounded suspiciously like an alcoholic drink to Lucy, and Mary had been about to order one!

"Good for you guys!" Delia said. "I just don't have the willpower."

"With Lucy around," Mary said, "who needs willpower?"

"I do what I can," Lucy said dryly.

Delia laughed.

Is Delia even twenty-one? Lucy wondered. Well, that wasn't Lucy's business, but Mary was, and *Mary* certainly wasn't twenty-one!

Their drinks came, and the girls ordered their food. As they waited, Lucy asked Delia about art school.

Suddenly Delia grew serious as she talked about her studies and projects. Lucy was impressed. It was clear that Delia was really into her art.

Mary was right, Lucy thought as they chatted, *I do like her.* But Delia was also a little reckless. As she drank her Coconut Sling, she began to talk loudly.

Lucy glanced at Mary, but Mary was just listening to Delia and smiling.

Lucy shook her head. *Am I being too uptight?* she thought. She shifted uncomfortably in her chair. Jeremy's family had called her a Goody Two-shoes. Was that what she was?

Their food came, and Lucy was pleasantly surprised by how good it was. While they ate, Delia ordered a second Coconut Sling. Lucy glanced at Mary again.

Mary looked back at her. She didn't want to say anything with Delia sitting right in front of them, but inside she was thinking, *Grow up, Lucy!*

When the bill came, everyone fished around for their wallets.

"Oh my God," Delia said. She looked at the sisters guiltily. "I don't have a penny on me! I'm so sorry, I wasn't thinking. If you guys can cover me, I can get cash at an ATM as soon as we leave."

"Don't worry about it," Mary said to Delia. But inside she was cringing. Mary still didn't have any cash! Lucy had already paid for their cab from the airport, and now she was going to have to pay for everyone's dinner! *Not good,* Mary thought, irritated with herself. How was she going to get Lucy to relax when she kept dropping the ball?

Lucy stared at Mary for a minute, then said, "Great." She checked the bill again, then started to fish twenties out of her wallet.

Delia looked pained. She cast an imploring look at Mary.

Mary sighed. "Wait," she said. "Let me put it on my credit card."

Lucy paused. "When did you get a credit card?"

"When I was in Buffalo," Mary responded. She hailed the waitress and handed her the bill and her credit card.

"Do Mom and Dad know you have one?" Lucy asked.

Mary shrugged. "Why do they need to?"

"Oh, because you might accumulate debt that they could end up being responsible for," Lucy answered.

"That won't happen," Mary said. "I pay off my bill every month."

"Maybe so far," Lucy said.

Delia groaned. "Will you two stop it?" she asked. "If I'd known you were going to bicker so much, I'd never have allowed you to stay with me!"

She smiled at them, but Lucy and Mary continued glaring across the table at each other.

The waitress returned. Mary signed the bill, and they left. They stood outside the restaurant for a moment, buttoning up their coats. It had gotten even colder, but in that nice autumn way, cold and sharp. If only they were wearing heavier coats!

Across the street a group of kids laughed and talked as they walked to the avenue. Somewhere nearby Lucy thought she could hear church bells chiming.

"Well, what do you girls want to do?" Delia asked. She had a mischievous look in her eye.

"I'm pretty tired—" Lucy began.

"Let's go out," Mary interrupted.

"Where do you want to go?" Delia asked.

Mary looked at Lucy. "I don't know. Somewhere loud?"

Delia's face lit up. "I've the perfect place!" she said. "What do you say, Lucy? I mean, I know you're tired. . . ."

Lucy sighed. In her head she could hear Jeremy: *Goody Two-shoes!* She forced a smile. "I'll be okay," she said. "We're only here for one night. Got to take advantage of it, right?"

"That's the spirit!" Delia said. "Follow me!"

She turned and headed down the street. Mary and Lucy followed right behind.

"You're such a jerk sometimes!" Lucy said under her breath, irritated with her sister for suggesting they go out.

"Sometimes you deserve it!" Mary said right back, feeling just as irritated.

They tramped down the street and turned up the avenue. Delia happily led the way. As they walked, she told them they were going to a cool new place called Sparticus. "And I just happen to know the doorman, so we'll get in for free!"

"How much is it usually?" Mary asked.

"You don't want to know," Delia said.

I guess that's one good thing about this, Lucy thought, *since I'm the only one with money!* Lucy noticed that Delia had forgotten all about going to the ATM.

After a ten-minute walk through the Village, they turned down a side street and came to a plain, gray building. There were no lights out front; there wasn't even a sign. The only way you'd know there was a club there was the line of people standing in front of the door, behind a velvet rope. At the front of the rope stood a very large, very round guy with his arms crossed.

"*That's* your friend?" Mary asked.

"Uh-huh. Come on!"

Delia led them past the line, right up to the big guy. He took one look at Delia and swept her up in his arms.

"Delia!" he boomed. "Where ya been?

I've been missing the sight of your pretty face."

Delia laughed. "How is it tonight?"

The doorman shrugged. "Okay. Who's this?" he asked, nodding at the Camdens.

"These are my friends Mary and Lucy. They're just visiting," Delia explained.

"I'm Rock," the big man said. He unclipped the velvet rope across the door and held it aside. "Ladies, enjoy your evening."

"Thanks, Rock," Mary said as she and Delia scooted past. She glanced back at the line of waiting people. She couldn't help but feel a thrill as they got in ahead of them all. And thanks to Delia, they hadn't even been asked for ID!

Inside, things were jumping. The music was incredibly loud; Mary felt each beat pulsing through her entire body. The place was dark, and packed full of people. Everybody was talking and laughing. Farther back in the room, Mary could see people dancing the night away. Mary grinned. There was something so *liberating* about places like this. It was so exciting! How could Lucy not get that?

She looked at her sister and wasn't surprised to see that Lucy was frowning. Lucy stripped off her hat, coat, and scarf.

Good idea! Mary thought. It was hot! Just inside the door was a girl hanging up coats in a long closet. They left their coats with her, then looked around.

"Where'd Delia go!" Lucy shouted at Mary. She had to yell to be heard over the music.

"What?" Mary shouted back.

Lucy leaned in closer to Mary. "Delia!" she shouted. "Where is she?"

Mary lifted her hands. "Don't know!" she shouted. "Isn't this place great?"

Lucy gave her sister a skeptical look. "Yeah, if you want to lose your hearing!"

"What?" Mary asked.

Lucy just shook her head. "Forget it!"

They stood there and checked over the crowd. Everyone was dressed in dark, expensive-looking clothes and smoking up a storm. Lucy coughed and made a face. She felt like she couldn't even breathe!

Suddenly Delia appeared in a break in the crowd. She made her way toward them, carrying three bottles of beer!

Lucy grabbed Mary's arm. "You're not

drinking, are you?" she yelled.

"So what if I do?" she yelled back. "Who cares?"

"I can think of two people in particular who'd care!" Lucy yelled, thinking of their mother and father.

"Hey!" Delia said as she came up to them. "I don't know what you guys like, so I just got my usual. I hope that's okay."

Delia passed a beer to Mary, then held the other one out for Lucy.

"No thanks!" Lucy said. "But let me pay you back for it!"

Delia shook her head. "It was free!" she said. "I know one of the bartenders!"

When Lucy looked surprised, Delia explained, "I come here a lot!" She put down the beer she'd brought for Lucy and lifted up the other one. "Cheers!" she yelled.

Mary clinked bottles with her; she and Lucy watched as Delia drained half the bottle in one gulp.

"Woohoo!" Delia yelled. "Let's go dance!"

Lifting her beer in the air, Delia sashayed through the crowd toward the dance floor.

Mary looked Lucy right in the eye and lifted her beer.

"Mary!"

Ignoring her sister, Mary tilted her beer back and took a sip.

Lucy's face reddened with anger. Before she could say anything, Mary shoved the bottle into her hand. "It was just a sip! You can throw it out, Pollyanna!"

Lucy just shook her head. "Didn't you learn *anything* in Buffalo?" she yelled. "It's *illegal* for you to drink!"

Mary poked her sister in the chest. "I feel *sorry* for you," she yelled. "You don't know how to relax and have a good time. Have a nice life!"

Then Mary turned and followed Delia out to the dance floor.

Lucy looked down at the beer in her hand. What her sister said hurt, but she knew that that bottle of beer didn't hold the answer. She put it down on a nearby table and sat down at the bar to wait.

FOUR

Three hours and a couple of Cokes later, Lucy was fuming. She'd been hit on by three or four drunk men and had breathed in so much secondhand smoke that she felt like she'd smoked a pack of cigarettes herself. At least the bartender was nice. She'd served Lucy her second Coke for free.

At the other end of the bar, Lucy watched Mary chat with some guy. *He's actually cute, and doesn't seem drunk!* Lucy thought, irritated. As she watched, Mary kissed the guy lightly, gave him a big smile, then turned and made her way over to Lucy.

"How's it going?" she asked.

"Great!" Lucy said. "Can't you tell? I'm having a great time!"

"I'm sorry for what I said before!" Mary said. "It was mean. I didn't mean it!"

"Yes you did," Lucy retorted.

"Okay, maybe I did, but just a little bit!" said Mary.

"It's okay," Lucy said. "I still think you're wrong!"

Mary rolled her eyes. "I'll be twenty-one soon anyway, but I promise not to drink again before then, okay?"

"So who was that guy?" Lucy asked.

Mary shrugged. "Just some guy," she answered. "Wasn't he cute?"

Lucy shrugged. "If you like that kind of guy, sure!"

"You mean the cute kind?" Mary asked.

Lucy laughed in spite of herself.

"So, are you ready to go?" Mary asked.

Lucy pretended to think about it. "I suppose I've had my fill of New York night-life."

Mary smiled. "Okay. I'll go find Delia."

One hour and another Coke later, Lucy was still waiting. Finally, she saw Mary making her way to the bar.

"What happened?" Lucy asked.

"I couldn't find her!" Mary said.

"It took you an hour to look for her?" Lucy asked.

Mary looked down. "Well, I ran into some cute guys. . . ."

"Oh, brother!"

Just then the bartender came over to them. "Hey! Are you ladies here with Delia?"

"Yeah!" Mary said.

"I thought you should know, she's passed out in the bathroom," the bartender said.

Oh my God! Lucy thought.

"Where is it!" Mary asked.

The bartender pointed toward the back of the club, and Mary and Lucy started winding their way through the crowd. At the back they found a line of guys waiting to use the men's room, and a bunch of girls clustered around the open door to the ladies'.

Lucy and Mary pushed through and found Delia lying on her side on the floor.

"Delia!" Mary said, crouching down beside her.

Delia's eyes fluttered open. "Mary!" she said. Her speech was slurred. "Just taking a little break."

Lucy was shocked. Delia had drunk so much, she couldn't even stand up!

Mary looked up at Lucy. "Help me get her up," she said.

Lucy knelt down. Together, she and Mary lifted the girl to her feet and started walking her back out through the club. When they got outside, Lucy helped Mary prop Delia up against the wall, then ran back inside to get their coats. When she got back outside, she found Mary supporting Delia as she threw up on the side of the street.

Oh, no! Lucy thought. She hurried over and took Mary's place as Mary put on her scarf and coat. Then they helped Delia put on hers. Then, with Delia propped up between them, they started down the street. All Lucy could think about was her friend Tanya, who'd drunk so much alcohol at their winter dance that they'd had to take her to the hospital. That had been a terrible, scary experience, and now it was happening again!

"Should we find a hospital?" Lucy asked her sister, shaking her head to clear it. Her ears were ringing, and it was hard to hear.

Mary sighed. "Believe it or not, I've seen Delia worse than this."

"You're kidding!" Lucy said.

"I wish I were," said Mary. While Mary liked to have a good time, Delia took things way too far.

Lucy looked sadly at the girl stumbling along beside her. Delia had only herself to blame for her wretched condition. Still, Lucy felt concerned for her.

"She'll be fine," Mary reassured Lucy. "We just need to get her home."

Home . . . Lucy jerked to a stop. "Do you know where we're going?" she asked.

"Don't you remember?" Mary asked, genuinely surprised.

Lucy looked incredulously at Mary. "Me?!? *You're* the one who set this up. Don't *you* remember where Delia lives?"

Mary shifted uncomfortably. "That's why I wrote it down on that piece of paper, so I wouldn't have to remember."

"And that piece of paper—" Lucy began.

"Is in my bag back at Delia's," Mary finished.

Lucy felt herself getting angry. *That won't help,* she told herself. *Keep it cool.*

She ducked her head to look into

Delia's face. Her eyes were half-lidded and her mouth was hanging open.

"Delia!" Lucy called. "Delia? Can you hear me? Where do you live? What's your address?"

Delia licked her lips and mumbled something.

"What?" Lucy asked. "Say it again."

But it looked like Delia had passed out.

Lucy looked at Mary. "Is there anyone you could call that would know her address?"

Mary was shaking her head. "I don't think so," she said. "I wouldn't know their phone numbers anyway."

"Well, we could call directory assistance. . . . That's it!" said Lucy. "Directory assistance! Do you see a pay phone?"

Lucy glanced around, and for the first time noticed their surroundings. The street was deserted. At least, it *seemed* to be. It was too dark to say for sure. The shadows she saw farther down the street could have been garbage cans . . . or people crouched down, waiting to mug them.

Lucy felt fear shoot through her. She was on a New York City street, it was after midnight, and she was lost.

Mary noticed her sister's anxiety. "Hey!" she said. "Don't worry. We're going to be all right. Let's go find a phone."

Supporting Delia between them, they walked to the corner. Halfway there, Mary saw a glowing pay-phone booth and pointed it out to her sister. Lucy kept her eyes on it and tried to ignore the shifting shadows all around them.

When they got to the pay phone, Lucy helped Mary prop Delia up against a wall, then went to the phone and dialed 411 for local information.

She got a message that information was no longer a free call; it now cost thirty-five cents.

Lucy slammed down the receiver.

Behind her, she heard Delia getting sick again. It was a terrible sound. She waited for it to be over, then turned and walked back to her sister. Mary was supporting her friend and gently wiping her mouth with Delia's coat sleeve.

"I need change," Lucy said to Mary. "It's not a free call."

"I don't have any," Mary said.

"Neither do I," said Lucy.

Lucy glanced around. The pay phone

she'd been trying to use was in front of a deli. Light blazed out from its windows. It was still open! *God bless New York for all-night delis*, Lucy thought.

She turned to Mary. "I'm going to go in there and get change."

"Good idea," Mary said. Delia took a deep breath and leaned back into Mary. She seemed to be asleep.

"Are you sure she's going to be okay?" Lucy asked.

Mary nodded. "Will you?" she asked her sister.

Lucy smiled. "I'll have to be. Hold on, I'll be right back."

"Hey!" Mary called after her. Lucy turned. "See if you can get a few napkins? I'd like to use something *other* than a coat sleeve to wipe Delia's mouth!"

"I'll see what I can do."

When she opened the door of the store, a bell chimed somewhere. The place was well lit, which made her feel better. A radio was tuned to a talk station. Someone was talking in a foreign language.

Next to the door was the cash register. An Asian man was standing there. He didn't look at Lucy when she came in.

"Excuse me?" Lucy said.

The guy looked at her but didn't say anything.

"Um . . . my friend is sick, and I need to use the pay phone, but I don't have any change. I was wondering . . ." Lucy proffered up a one-dollar bill. "Could I get change?"

"You buy something first," the man said.

"I have to buy something?"

"Yeah. You buy something, I give you change." He nodded at the variety of snacks and gum displayed in front of the cash register.

"Um . . ." Lucy looked them over and quickly grabbed a health bar.

The guy rang it up. "A dollar thirty-nine," he said.

"Oh," Lucy said. She opened her wallet and got out another dollar.

The guy took the two dollars and gave her change.

"Thanks," Lucy said.

The man grunted and turned his attention back to the radio.

Nice guy, Lucy thought, pushing through the door.

"How'd it go?" Mary asked.

"Okay," Lucy said. "I got the change."

"What about the napkins?" Mary asked.

She'd forgotten the napkins! Lucy looked back in the store. She could see napkins stacked next to the cash register. Without saying a word she turned and walked back into the store.

"Mind if I grab some of these?" she asked the guy. Before he could respond she snagged a few off the top. "Thanks!"

Phew! Lucy thought with a grin. *That's better.*

She handed the napkins to Mary, then went to the phone and slipped in the change. This time her call to 411 went through, and she got Delia's address.

"167 East 7th Street, apartment 7A," Lucy said.

Mary stood up, and Lucy hurried over to help with Delia. They got their bearings, then started their trek home.

FIVE

Lucy opened her eyes and immediately closed them again. She raised her hand to shield them from the glaring sun and opened them again. For a moment, she didn't know where she was. On the wall opposite where she was sleeping was a collection of paintings of flowers with the most vivid colors. . . .

Suddenly everything that had happened the night before came crashing back. Lucy groaned. *What a nightmare!*

After getting back to the apartment and putting Delia to bed, Lucy and Mary had collapsed on the futon. Lucy sighed and closed her eyes again. *At least it's over,* she thought. *Today we leave for Buffalo and return to normalcy.*

Lucy sat bolt upright in bed. Last night she'd been too tired to even take her clothes off. She looked at her watch in a panic. It was twelve-thirty in the afternoon—and their train to Buffalo left Penn Station at one o'clock!

"Mary!" Lucy said. She pushed her sister's shoulder.

"Uh," Mary said.

"Mary, get up!" Lucy shouted. She jumped out of bed, glad now that she hadn't taken off her clothes the night before. Their bags were still sitting unopened in the middle of the floor.

We can be out of here in five minutes, Lucy thought. *We can make it!*

When Lucy thought of missing this train and having to spend another moment in the city . . .

"Mary! We're going to miss the train to Buffalo. Get up!"

Mary turned and shielded her eyes. "What train?"

Lucy was putting on her shoes. She tossed Mary's at her head. "We've got to get out of here. Now!"

"Ugh," Mary said. She sat up and groaned. "What happened last night?"

"It'll come back to you," Lucy said. She stood up. "I'm going to go check on Delia. Then we're leaving."

Mary nodded and rubbed her face.

Lucy walked down the hall to Delia's room. Last night they'd stumbled back here without any lights. Lucy was glad. In the light of day it was disgusting. The tiny kitchen was back here, and it was just as bad as Lucy had feared. Unwashed dishes were piled in the sink, and the counters were absolutely grungy.

Don't look at it, Lucy thought, sidling by. Delia had a small bedroom at the back of the apartment.

"Delia," Lucy called, flicking on the light. Being careful not to jar Delia, Lucy sat down on the bed.

"Delia," she said again, softly. She touched the girl's shoulder. Delia groaned.

"Lucy?"

"Yeah. How are you feeling?"

"Terrible," Delia said. She slowly turned over and squinted at Lucy. "Hey!" she said with a smile.

Lucy smiled back. "Hey."

"So did we have fun last night, or what?" Delia asked.

Lucy laughed. "If that's your idea of fun . . ."

Delia groaned and closed her eyes. "I feel terrible. You'd think as many times as I do that, I'd learn my lesson."

"Can I get you any aspirin or anything?" Lucy asked. "Mary and I have got to run to catch a train."

"No, I'll be okay," Delia said. "But thanks. By the way, what happened last night? The last thing I remember is dancing at Spartacus and feeling like I was going to be sick. I remember heading in the direction of the bathroom and then . . ."

Delia shrugged.

Lucy rubbed Delia's arm. "You got a little sick."

"Oh, no," Delia said. "Was I a lot of trouble?"

Lucy smiled again. "It wasn't too bad."

"Liar," Delia said. "I'm sorry, Lucy. I just wanted to show you girls a good time."

"Don't worry about it," Lucy said. She paused, then said, "You know, Mary and I were really worried about you last night.

You scared us; you were *really* sick."

"I know," Delia said.

"I have an aunt who's a recovering alcoholic," Lucy went on. "She's doing better now, but for a while there . . . drinking almost ruined her life."

Delia lowered her eyes and didn't say anything.

"I mean," Lucy went on, "social drinking by someone who's of legal drinking age is one thing—"

"Oh, I'm twenty-one," Delia interjected. "Didn't Mary tell you?"

"It didn't come up," Lucy said. "But still, you blacked out last night! And today you can't remember anything that happened!"

"I know," Delia said again.

Lucy sighed. "It would make me feel better if I thought you were going to get help."

Delia didn't say anything.

"She's right," Mary said from behind them. Lucy turned and found Mary standing in the doorway with her jacket on and her bag over her shoulder. "I mean, Lucy can be a bit of a puritan. . . ."

Lucy opened her mouth to object, but Mary motioned for her to be quiet. "But this happens to you too frequently, Delia. It isn't good."

Delia sighed. "Maybe you're right," she said.

"We are right," said Mary. "I'll call you when we get back home to see how you're doing."

Delia smiled. "Thanks, gals."

"Now get out of here," Delia said. "I think I'll just sleep a little longer. . . ."

Lucy and Mary laughed. "Talk to you soon," Mary said. Lucy stood up and turned out the light, then she and her sister hurried down the hall and out the apartment door.

Rather than wait for the elevator, they bounded down Delia's stairs and out the front door. It was a beautiful day outside. It had warmed up a little, and the sun was shining brightly.

Lucy stepped to the curb and hailed a taxi. They piled in, bags and all.

"Penn Station," Lucy said breathlessly. The driver nodded and hit the meter. A recorded voice came on welcoming them to New York City and encouraging them to buckle up.

Good advice, Lucy thought. She slid over and put on the shoulder seat belt. Mary did the same on the other side. The girls sat back and caught their breath. Lucy glanced at her watch. They had fifteen minutes before their train left. Lucy couldn't remember where exactly the station was, but she thought it was on the West Side in the thirties.

Their driver turned off Delia's street onto an avenue. They sped quickly along that road, and Lucy thought they'd get to the train station with plenty of time to spare. But as soon as the driver turned onto a street to go across town, their progress slowed to a crawl. By the time they pulled up to Penn Station, it was one o'clock on the dot.

Lucy already had her money out. She paid the driver and vaulted out of the cab. "Let's go!" she said to Mary. *We are* not *missing this train!* she thought.

They hurried down steps to the underground train station. Before them was a long, wide hallway with shops on either side. Mary and Lucy flew down the hall, dodging slower-moving people as they went.

In the main room of the station was a large board with all the train times and gate numbers. Their train was right at the top. Under notes it said ALL ABOARD. Lucy checked the gate.

"It's Gate 14," she said. "Come on!"

The sisters hurried to the gate and rushed down the escalator to another sub-level where the tracks were. They got to the bottom of the escalator just in time to see the last car of their train pull away from the platform.

Lucy threw down her bag in frustration. Behind her, Mary let out a long breath. "I can't believe we missed it," she said.

Lucy whirled around. "Really? I'm surprised, since you did everything you could last night to be sure we would!"

"Oh, come on!" Mary said. "It's not all my fault."

Lucy turned her back to her sister and just shook her head. She was too angry to speak. She tried to focus on what to do next. *We'll need to call the Colonel and tell him we missed the train,* Lucy thought, *and check when the next one is.*

That's the next step, she thought. *When is the next train?* With any luck it would be just an hour or two from now, and they could just wait at the station.

They weren't lucky. There were trains to Buffalo all day, but, because of heavy holiday traffic, the seats were all booked. There wasn't any space available until the next day!

Lucy converted the tickets they had to ones for tomorrow's train, then called the Colonel collect to give him their new information.

"Are you two okay?" he wanted to know.

"We're fine," Lucy assured him. "At least now we have more time to explore the city!"

"That's putting a good face on it!" the Colonel said.

If you only knew, Lucy thought. She hung up and went to find Mary, who was standing with their bags, right under the main board. It looked like she was asleep on her feet.

"Oh, no you don't," Lucy said.

"Huh?" said Mary. "What happened?"

"No sleeping for you," said Lucy. "Since we're stuck here for another day, we're going to do what *I* want to do."

Mary was awake enough to sneer. "Oh, great. *That* sounds like fun. I bet you want to do all the typical tourist stuff, like going to the top of the Empire State Building."

"Maybe," said Lucy. "The only rule is: *You* don't get to complain."

Mary ducked her head guiltily. "Fine," she said. "I guess I owe you."

"And as much as I hate to say it, I think we need to stay with Delia again tonight. Why don't you give her a call?"

"She probably won't pick up," Mary said.

"I'm sure she won't," said Lucy. "Just leave a message."

After Mary made the call, the girls left the station and, still toting their bags, walked up to the street. Lucy took a deep breath. It really *was* a beautiful day, and it was all theirs to do with as they pleased!

"So, what do you want to do?" Mary asked.

"Well . . . ," Lucy said. "I always wanted to go skating at Rockefeller Center, but never found the time when I was living here."

Mary made a face. "Ice-skating? At Rockefeller Center? Could you *be* any more of a tourist?"

Lucy held up her finger. "You're forgetting the rule: You don't get to complain."

Mary pressed her lips together.

"Good," said Lucy. "Now the question is, how do we get there? I *think* it's pretty close by."

"Permission to speak?" Mary asked.

"Granted," Lucy said.

"We could just ask someone," Mary said.

Lucy smiled. She was feeling good enough to do just that. They stopped a man in a business suit, who paused for just a moment, then, without smiling, pointed them in the right direction and continued on his way.

"Wow," Lucy said. "So sorry to have bothered him."

"Hey, this is New York," Mary said. "Places to go, people to see!"

The girls laughed and started walking. The Rink at Rock Center was pretty crowded when they got there. It was only a few days before Thanksgiving, after all. The city was full of tourists, and, Lucy admitted to herself, Mary had been right. Rockefeller Center was a big tourist attraction.

"Hey, look!" Mary said. "The tree is up!"

Although it wasn't lit yet, the Christmas tree that went up every year at Rock Center was in place.

"It's *huge!*" Lucy said.

"So do you want to skate, or what?" Mary asked.

They walked down to the rink area. The air was noticeably cooler down there, but Lucy thought it felt exciting in a holiday kind of way. The sisters stowed their shoes and bags in lockers, rented skates, and made their way out to the ice.

Once on the ice, Lucy's spirits rose again. She zoomed twice around the rink. It was on her third circuit that someone dressed in all blue, with a white cloth saying SAFETY PATROL on his chest, whistled at her and motioned for her to slow down.

Lucy blushed. "Sorry!" she called.

"That's okay," the guy said, smiling. "Just slow it down a little bit."

Chagrined, Lucy looked around for

Mary. Mary was still near the side of the rink, just tottering along. Lucy skated over to her.

"That was embarrassing," she said.

Mary laughed. "And you think *I'm* too wild."

Lucy laughed, then said, "Sorry. I forgot you don't really skate."

Mary shrugged. "Hey, no problem. Today we do what you want to do."

Lucy grinned at her sister. "Thanks," she said. She took Mary's arm and helped her away from the wall. "Why don't you let me give you a little skating lesson. . . ."

SIX

Mary and Lucy skated for a couple of hours. By the time they were ready to call it quits, it was starting to get dark.

"Well," Mary said, as they returned their skates, "it's getting late. What else do you want to do?"

"Times Square," Lucy said, "definitely."

"Times Square it is," Mary said. They walked to the famous tourist stop. Lucy had passed through the area when she'd lived in New York, but never stopped to take a look. The sisters wandered down Broadway with their faces to the sky, admiring all the billboards, signs, and TV screens.

"Amazing," Mary said.

"It really is," Lucy breathed.

The girls were so involved in the sights and sounds of Times Square that they weren't really looking where they were going. So when someone slammed into them from behind, they were taken totally by surprise.

The girls went flying! Lucy looked up to see a kid running away from them—and he had her purse!

A thief! Lucy thought. "Hey!" she yelled. "That guy's got my purse!"

In a flash Mary was back up on her feet and sprinting after the guy. He was small and quick, but Mary was fast. She was gaining on him when she dodged around someone and ran full speed into a guy her age. They bounced off each other and collapsed to the ground.

"Hey!" the guy said.

Mary pointed after the thief. "That guy stole my sister's purse," she panted.

"What?" said another guy standing beside them. "I'll be right back!" he said, and sprinted off after the thief.

The guy Mary had run into stood up

and offered Mary his hand. Mary took it, and he helped her to her feet. "Are you okay?" he asked.

Mary nodded, still breathing hard.

The guy shook his head. He had dark hair, cut very short, and dark eyes. *Ooh,* Mary thought. *This guy is hot!*

"I can't believe I just saw that," he said. "That kind of thing never happens here anymore. Are you sure you're okay?"

"Yeah," she said. "Thanks. I can't believe your friend went after the guy."

"I only hope he catches him," he said. "My name's Scott, by the way."

"Nice to run into you," Mary said with a smile. "Mary."

"Nice to be run into by you," said Scott, holding on to Mary's hand.

"Hey! What happened?" Lucy asked as she ran up to them.

Mary introduced Scott to Lucy and explained what had happened. Right away, Lucy noticed the chemistry between Scott and Mary. She smiled to herself. *Definitely Mary's type,* she thought.

Then Scott's friend appeared out of the crowd. He was dangling Lucy's purse by the strap and smiling.

"You got it!" Lucy said. "I can't believe it! Thank you so much!"

"My pleasure," Scott's friend said. He had wavy blond hair and piercing blue eyes.

Cute! Lucy thought.

"I was about to grab the guy when he dropped the purse," Scott's friend said. "So it's not like I did anything particularly heroic. My name's Jeremy, by the way."

Lucy and Mary looked at each other, shocked. *Jeremy?!*

They shook hands, and Lucy chuckled to herself. *As if there's only one Jeremy in all of New York City.* Still, it was a little weird.

"We're roommates," Jeremy said. "We're both in our first jobs out of college. What about you two?"

Taking turns, Mary and Lucy related what had happened to them last night.

"Wow!" Scott said, laughing. "That sounds like one tough night!"

Jeremy just shook his head.

"Listen," Scott said, "we can't let you leave New York City with only that experience of the nightlife. Why don't you let Jeremy and me take you two out tonight."

"That's a *great* idea," Jeremy said. "What do you say?"

Mary looked at Lucy. Lucy realized that Mary was leaving it up to her. Lucy smiled. "I think it sounds like a wonderful idea."

"Me, too," said Mary.

The guys both grinned. "Great! So shall we pick you up at this Delia's place, say around eight o'clock?" Jeremy asked.

"Sounds good," Lucy said. They said their farewells, and Lucy and Mary hailed a cab back to Delia's apartment.

"So far, little sister," Mary said after they'd stowed their bags in the trunk and climbed in, "I'm liking your day a lot better than mine."

SEVEN

When they got back, Delia was still nursing her hangover. They found her lying on the couch, staring at the TV.

Delia apologized again about the night before. "I can't remember a thing, and that in itself means I *must* have been a basket case."

"It wasn't the *best* time I've ever had going out," Mary agreed, "but tonight promises to be a different story. . . ."

The sisters told Delia about their day, the theft of Lucy's purse, and running into Jeremy and Scott.

"Oh my God!" Delia said. "It's so romantic! Have an incredible time."

"Do you want to come?" Lucy offered.

"I feel a little stupid going out without you and then coming back here to stay the night."

Delia turned down the invitation. "I appreciate it, but I'm not quite ready to be up and about. Besides, four's company, five's a crowd."

The sisters tucked all their bags in a corner of the room, then took turns in the bathroom. To Lucy the bathroom looked like it hadn't been cleaned *ever,* but she was too happy to be taking a shower to let it worry her.

Promptly at eight o'clock, the buzzer rang. "Tell them we'll meet them downstairs!" Lucy called.

Before they left, Delia gave them a set of keys. The sisters thanked her and headed out.

The boys were waiting for them outside. They both looked great in dark jeans, sweaters, and dark leather jackets. The air was crisp and clear. It was a beautiful night.

"Ladies," Jeremy greeted them. Jeremy took Lucy's arm, and Scott took Mary's. They started down the street.

"Where are we going?" Lucy asked.

"Why don't you let us worry about that," Jeremy said. "But we intend to show you that you don't have to go somewhere loud to have a good time."

"Hey!" Mary said.

Scott grinned. "Not that there isn't a time and place for everything."

"Thank you," Mary said, mollified.

The two couples took a leisurely stroll through the East Village. *Am I imagining things, or am I getting used to this?* Lucy thought. There was something about the openness of the people they passed that created a casual, warm feeling on the street.

After a while the guys stopped them in front of a wooden door. A sign above the door said RACHEL'S. Scott opened the door for them, and Jeremy gestured for the girls to go in first.

Inside they found a long room full of small, circular tables. At the far end of the room was a low stage. Sitting on a stool on the stage, playing an acoustic guitar and singing, was a girl with long black hair. The people at the tables were talking softly, eating, and listening to the girl perform.

"Wow," Lucy said.

"This is one of our favorite places," Jeremy said.

"Who performs here?" Mary asked.

Scott shrugged. "Anybody. It's almost always open mike, though sometimes they book people, too."

Jeremy was chatting with the hostess; it seemed they knew each other. She led them toward the front of the room. As they walked through, Jeremy and Scott said hello to several people.

They sat down at a table near the stage, and the hostess gave them menus. Almost immediately, a waiter appeared. "Can I get you anything to drink?" he asked.

Mary immediately spoke up. "I'll have a Coke," she said.

"Make it two," said Lucy.

Scott spread his hands. "Cokes all around?"

Jeremy nodded.

As they looked over the menu, Lucy couldn't contain her curiosity. "Who were those people you were talking to?" she asked.

"Oh, just people we know from work," Jeremy said. "Scott and I work at MTV, in video production."

"Actually," Scott said, "we're assistants to video producers."

Jeremy grinned. "We're just getting started."

Mary was looking around. "So a lot of people from MTV come here?"

Jeremy nodded. "It tends to be an 'industry' crowd," he said with a smile.

"As in, the music industry?" Mary asked.

Jeremy nodded again.

Mary turned to Lucy and mouthed, "Cool!"

Dinner was wonderful. The food was called tapas, and the group chose a lot of small dishes to share. There was everything from lamb kebobs to mussels to roasted pepper salad. But if the food was good, the company was even better! Lucy couldn't believe they'd been so lucky to run into such interesting guys. As they ate, they talked and listened to the various performers. Most were singer/songwriters with just a guitar, but a couple of people got up and recited poetry they had written. One guy even tried out a comedy routine!

As they talked, it came to light that both Lucy and Mary had sung before. The guys looked at each other. "I think we'll need a demonstration," Scott said.

"I wholeheartedly agree!" said Jeremy. "The evening wouldn't be complete without a performance from you two!"

"Oh, no," Lucy said. "There's no way—"

"I don't know," Mary said thoughtfully. She looked at Lucy. "It might be fun. . . ."

But once again, Lucy could tell that Mary was willing to let her decide. Lucy gave her sister a big grin.

"Well . . . what would we sing?"

Mary shrugged. "The question is, what *can* we sing?"

Lucy thought for a moment. "Something by Peter, Paul, and Mary?"

Mary made a face. "I was thinking more like Alanis Morissette."

Lucy snapped her fingers. "The Indigo Girls!"

" 'Closer to Fine'?" Mary suggested.

Lucy nodded her head. "That's perfect!"

Jeremy nodded. "Hold on a minute," he said, and got up from the table.

Lucy turned to Mary. "Are we really going to do this?"

"Why not?" Mary said. "It'll be fun!"

Lucy looked at Scott. "I'm nervous!" she said.

Scott smiled. "Don't be," he said.

Suddenly the hostess was onstage, asking for everyone's attention. "Ladies and gentlemen, we have guests from out of town who'd like to perform a song for you. Let's give a warm welcome to Mary and Lucy Camden!"

There was scattered applause around the room. Jeremy slipped back into his seat. "You're on!" he said.

Mary stood up. "Let's go!" she said, giving Lucy a big smile.

Lucy grabbed her sister's hand and walked up to the stage with her. The hostess welcomed them. "Are you singing without a guitar?" she asked.

"I guess so," Mary said.

"Well, we can't have that," she said, scanning the crowd. She gestured to someone, and before they knew what was happening, the dark-haired girl they'd seen when they first came in was sitting with them with her guitar.

"Whenever you guys are ready," she said.

Mary looked at Lucy. *Ready?* she seemed to be asking. Lucy smiled and nodded.

The guitarist played a little of the song for them, as a lead-in. Then Mary launched into the song. After a moment, Lucy joined her, tentatively singing the harmonies. But before long, Lucy had forgotten about the audience and was just enjoying singing. She and Mary belted it out, like they would have in their old bedroom in Glenoak.

When they finished, the place erupted! "Want to do another one?" the guitarist asked.

"Let's quit while we're ahead," Lucy said.

"Whatever you say," Mary said. Waving to the crowd, they returned to their seats.

Jeremy and Scott were blown away. "Wow!" Scott said. He shook his head. "Wow!"

"It's obvious that you're sisters," Jeremy said. "You sound really nice together."

Lucy and Mary smiled at each other. They linked arms. "Yeah, we do, don't we?" said Mary.

"Sister," Lucy said, and gave Mary's arm a squeeze.

EIGHT

Jeremy and Scott walked them home to Delia's apartment. Out front they exchanged addresses and phone numbers.

"If you're ever in the city again, don't hesitate to give us a call," Scott said.

"We won't," said Mary.

"Thanks for a wonderful evening," Lucy said.

Each couple kissed good night, then Mary and Lucy let themselves into Delia's building with the keys she'd given them. Upstairs, Delia was in bed, asleep.

The next morning, Lucy and Mary got up with plenty of time to make their train. After cleaning up, they said goodbye to

Delia and caught a cab to the station.

When they got there, Lucy was taking out her wallet to pay when Mary stopped her. "I've got this one," she said.

"You've got money?" Lucy asked.

Mary pulled out a wad of cash. "I made a sneak visit to the ATM this morning when you were in the shower."

Mary paid the cabdriver, and they went into the station. When the time came, they boarded their train and settled back for a leisurely trip to Buffalo. As she settled into her seat, Lucy reflected back on the past two days.

It was a success, she realized. Despite the rocky start—or maybe even partly because of it—Mary and she bonded, just as Lucy had hoped.

"Hey," Mary said, "I just wanted to tell you how much fun I had with you our second day. I was wrong when I said you didn't know how to have fun."

"No you weren't," Lucy said. "I *definitely* need to learn how to relax sometimes." She looked at her sister. "Even though I can be a jerk about it, I look to you to help me with that."

Mary grinned. "Maybe between the

two of us, we can figure out how to have fun *without* getting into trouble."

"I just realized something," Lucy said. "If it hadn't been for our crazy first night, if we'd gone home after eating like I'd wanted to, we wouldn't have missed the train and had that entire second day together."

Lucy looked at her sister. "If that first night was the price to pay for the second day, I'd pay it again, without thinking."

Mary smiled and shook her head. "Let's hope it doesn't come to that!"

They fell silent, looking out the window as the New York skyline disappeared from view. *Two amazing days,* Lucy thought. And it was just going to get better. Now they were on their way to the Colonel's house, to spend a holiday with family, at a place that had been Mary's home for a long time. Best of all, they were going together.

DON'T MISS THIS BRAND-NEW, ORIGINAL 7TH HEAVEN STORY

Coming June 2003!

MARY'S
RESCUE

Mary Camden is working as a lifeguard at a fabulous beach resort, and she's invited her siblings to visit her. What could be more perfect? But this idyllic resort town holds secrets. . . . First, Mary's friend disappears from the beach on her watch. Then Mary gets blamed for a burglary. Can the Camden kids get to the bottom of these mysteries and clear Mary's name?

Coming June 2003!
ISBN: 0-375-82409-X

DON'T MISS THIS EXCITING ORIGINAL 7TH HEAVEN STORY

Now Available!

CAMP
CAMDEN

Lucy and Ruthie are off to summer camp in sunny Malibu, California, where swimming, boating, and horseback riding aren't their only pastimes! Lucy's teaching a class that catches the attention of a handsome counselor, and Ruthie is pulling pranks that make everyone take notice! Meanwhile, back at the Camden house, Simon's trying his latest money-making scheme—day-trading on the Internet! But is the stock market ready for Simon Camden?